THE FALL

By Briuana Green

To my grandparents, Aunt Teresa, Aunt Marilyn, and Uncle Del, this book is dedicated to all of you.

Acknowledgments

Writing a book has been something that I have wanted to do ever since I was in the first grade. Now that I have my first book completed, I look back and remember the great people who have helped this book come to life.

To my parents, Mitchell and Tracey: thank you for always supporting my dreams. I really appreciate all of the sacrifices you two have made for me over the years, even when things were tough. I hope I've made you proud.

To my sister, Keyunna: thank you for providing me with endless laughter and for always being ready to do whatever it is you can to help me. You have inspired me in more ways than you know, and I cannot wait to see all of the great things that you will do in the future.

To one of my best friends, Evan: I am so glad that I always have you here. You have been the perfect listening ear, and you have been here since the early stages of this novel. Thank you for always encouraging me to think outside the box and reminding me to "just breathe" when times get hard.

To my BoPro sister, Sarah: I will be forever grateful for you agreeing to read my book. You were the first person to read what I had written, and your feedback was beyond helpful. You are greatly appreciated.

To one of my favorite authors, Celeste O. Norfleet: thank you for responding the first time I emailed you years ago. Your guidance throughout the years has made my journey much easier. If it wasn't for you, I'm sure this novel wouldn't be completed.

To my mentee, Kayla: thank you for believing in me when I couldn't even believe in myself. Having someone like you in my life is more than enough motivation. Please continue being an inspiration.

To my Salem Missionary Baptist Church Family: thank you for constantly being a major support system in my life. Having your endless encouragement whenever I come home from school has done wonders in my life.

To my Harvard Cheer Family: all of you are amazing! Thanks for giving me the motivation to be the best version of myself.

To my hometown, Forrest City: I would not be who I am or where I am today without you. No matter how far I go, I will never forget where I came from.

To the reader: thank you for supporting my dream. It is my prayer that this novel changes your life as much as it has changed mine through writing it. Always remember that you have a voice.

Most importantly, to my Lord and Savior: thank You for showing me the need for a novel like this. Thank You for providing me with the perfect outlet to all of the various emotions that I was feeling while writing this book. Thank You for giving me the strength to endure everything that I have gone through in life that has inspired many of the lessons in this book. You are awesome!

The Clique

Love

Love Skyy Hudson is a spiritual fifteen-year-old high school sophomore from Forrest City, Arkansas. She is a 5'2, African-American with brown eyes. She loves being versatile with her hair, sometimes wearing her big, curly, black afro and sometimes wearing various weaves. At her high school in Atlanta, Georgia, Martin Luther King High School AKA KHS, Love holds a 4.0 GPA and a coveted spot on the KHS cheerleading squad. She takes the most pride in being a child of God with a lovely voice that she uses to bless others. She is the daughter of Pastor Joseph Hudson, the pastor of Trinity Christian Center, and Mrs. Laila Hudson, a famous lawyer. She also has a big brother, Micah Hudson, who is a senior at KHS, and a twin sister Truth Hudson. Presently, Love is struggling with lack of confidence and shyness.

Truth

Truth Starr Hudson, twin sister of Love, is also a fifteen-year-old high school sophomore at KHS. She is 5'2, with long, black hair, and bright green eyes. Like her sister, Truth is a varsity cheerleader and is known for her beautiful voice. She is known at KHS for being very wild, outgoing, and headstrong, and she holds a 2.7 GPA. Currently, Truth is struggling to focus on God and her schoolwork due to boy drama.

Mercy

Mercy Perez is a 5'4, sixteen-year-old sophomore at KHS. She is an Afro-Latina, and she has long, curly, brown hair. Her big, gray eyes and outgoing personality makes her a favorite at KHS among both boys and girls. She is class president and the youngest captain in the history of KHS Cheerleading. Mercy holds a 3.5 GPA and is dating the star wide receiver of the KHS Panthers, Joel Jackson, a KHS senior. Dr. Matthew Perez, who doubles as a deacon at Trinity Christian Center, is her father. Dr. Rina Perez, the Advanced Placement Physics teacher at KHS, is her mother. Joy Perez, KHS senior, is Mercy's older sister. Mercy is struggling with family and peer pressure, haters in the school, her pride, and pursuing her faith in God.

Ava

Ava Lee is a 5'0, fifteen-year-old sophomore with short, black hair and deep black eyes at KHS. She is the best on the step team at school, and she holds a 2.5 GPA. Ava is the only daughter of Hoc Lee, CEO of Lee Enterprises, and Kim Lee, a stay-at-home mother. They are originally from South Korea. Ava is struggling with judgment from within the church, achieving success in school, and the fear of disappointing her family.

Ryann

Ryann Warner is a 5'7, Caucasian sophomore at KHS. She has long, red hair and green eyes. She is a varsity basketball player for KHS, and she holds a 2.0 GPA. Ryann's father ran off when she was only three years old, and her mother, Sarah Warner, works two different jobs to provide for her family. Ryann has three siblings: Reagan, a KHS freshman, Romeo, a KHS junior, and River, who is 9 years old. Ryann has the determined spirit of her mother, but she is struggling with money problems and her disbelief in God.

~ 1 ~

New Beginnings

"For I know the plans I have for you," says the Lord. "They are plans for good and not for disaster, to give you a future and a hope."

Jeremiah 29:11 NLT

Love

I'm bummed. After such a great summer, it's time for us to go to school. It's not like I hate school or anything, but I love the freedom summer brings. Summer is full of nothing but sunshine and good vibes, but all of this subsides when it's time for school to start again.

Last week, my family and I were in Florida for a last-minute getaway vacation. We stayed in a small, luxurious resort on the coast of Palm Beach called Coastal Diamonds Resort & Spa, and it was amazing. Just remembering the way the breeze felt blowing through my hair as I stared at the breathtaking view of the waters makes me wish I was still there. I also have a nice tan to remind me of my time spent in Florida.

As Micah, my older brother, pulls his black Mustang out of the driveway, thoughts of entering my sophomore year at Martin Luther King High School begin to overtake me. First days of school have always made me somewhat nervous because everything is so new, and you never know how things are going to turn out. There are new classes, new teachers, and new classmates that you have to become acclimated with.

I've been thinking a lot about college lately, despite the fact that I'm just beginning my sophomore year of high school. It's never too early to start planning for your future, but sometimes it can get a little overwhelming. There are a lot of great schools in Georgia and my old home state, Arkansas, that I would love to attend. However, I want to branch out of what is typically expected of a young, Black female and pursue an education at an Ivy League college like Harvard or somewhere. I know it's possible, and I would love to be the one to help others realize that it's possible for people like us.

"What's wrong with you, Love?" Micah eases toward a stop at the red light closest to our school.

"Nothing much. I'm just feeling butterflies," I reveal, dejectedly. "Plus, I'm thinking about where I want to go for college." Micah is a senior this year, so I bet he can relate to what I'm feeling right now.

I can't believe it's his last year of high school and that next year around this time he'll be heading to class as a young, college brother. A lot of big colleges are eyeing him as a potential quarterback for their football teams. He's six foot four and two hundred and twenty pounds of muscle, but he's also quick on his feet. Any team would be blessed to have him.

"You've got this, Love. I'm sure you've prayed about this year over a hundred times already. As long as you continue to put in the work, you'll be set when the time comes for you to apply to college," Micah says.

There are already throngs of students lining the sidewalks headed toward the school. A lot of these faces are ones I've never seen before. Maybe I should try to branch out this year and get to know more of my classmates. KHS is large school with over two thousand students. KHS is made of predominantly Black students, but there are also a lot of Whites, Asians, Latinos, and mixed-race students here too.

"Love, you worry too much," my twin sister, Truth, says. Truth's transition from junior high to high school was a lot easier than mine. She's the outgoing, outspoken, wild twin, and I'm the shy, quiet, and innocent one.

My closest friends are Mercy, Ava, Ryann, and my sister. All I really want to do is find my place at this school without compromising my Christian beliefs in the process. I feel like God is constantly trying to remind me that I was never born to fit in with this world, but it's difficult trying not to when this world is all you see.

The temptation to do what everyone else is doing to fit in is at an all-time high. People are swapping respect and morals just for attention, and that's not something I was ever comfortable doing.

"You're right, Truth. I don't know why I'm already letting my nerves get the best of me," I reply, attempting to laugh off my nervousness.

"You know your big bro has your back if you ever need anything. We're family and that's what family members do. If any chick steps to you in the wrong way, you have your twin to help you, but if any of the brothers here come at you period, I'll be there before you know it," Micah says as the overprotective side of him starts to come out. Because Micah is the oldest out of the three of us and he's a young man, he automatically feels like it's his job to watch over us and protect us as the older brother.

"Thanks, bro. I'm sure we already knew that," I sarcastically respond as Micah pulls into one of the senior parking spots closest to the school building. I guess priority parking is one of the many perks of being a senior at this school. I can't wait until I turn sixteen in a few months, so I can finally be able to get my license.

"Did you hear me?" Micah asks Truth.

He looks into his rearview mirror to get a glimpse of her face, but she is too busy on her phone to even notice. Between Facebook, Snapchat, Instagram, and Twitter, most of Truth's attention nowadays is taken up by social media. If social media doesn't have her attention, she's busy texting these guys who I like to call her "randoms" because they serve no real purpose in her life besides entertainment or whatever.

"Umm Truth?" I utter in an attempt to help her out before our brother goes ballistic. Being the middle child, I oftentimes find myself trying to mediate between the two of them. I know I'm only two minutes older than my sister, but sometimes I feel like those two minutes make a huge difference in the terms of our maturity levels.

"What?" Truth responds.

"Nothing, girl. Have a good day at school, and remember the reason you're here. Education first, everything else is secondary," says Micah as he checks for the time on his cell phone. We still have about fifteen minutes before the first bell rings.

"God first, then family, education, and everything else," I correct him.

"Amen!" Micah says.

God has to be the head of everything we do, and it is important that we don't get our priorities out of whack. That is something our parents have been communicating to us since the moment we were old enough to understand what they meant. Our parents didn't have much when they were growing up, and they remind us of it every chance they get. We are blessed to say we didn't have to go through any moments where we didn't have food in our stomachs or a roof over our heads like they did when they were our age. It is by the grace of God that we are able to enjoy the things we do today.

"Alright y'all. I'm about to go meet up with my boys before class. I'll see y'all after school. I love both of you, and have a good day," Micah says.

"I love you too," I respond.

"Love you too, big head!" Truth shouts as Micah begins to walk toward the school.

"Are you going to head out too, Truth?" I ask.

"Yeah, I'm about to meet Ryann. Ava said she'll catch up with us in class, and I think Mercy said she was riding with Joel," she replies, placing her iPhone in her brown, Michael Kors tote.

"Ok, that's cool. I'll meet up with you and Ava in class. I'm about to sit in the car and pray for a little bit," I respond, checking my fro in the mirror. My hair is one of the things I take pride in, and it also distinguishes me from my twin sister who loves for her long, black hair to be bone straight.

"Alright," Truth says as she exits the car. She has on a pretty pink sundress that goes well with her radiant, golden skin tone. I notice a lot of the guys standing outside of the school look pleased to see her strutting by, and I can understand why. My sister is gorgeous, and I'm not just saying that because we look exactly alike.

As Truth enters the school building, I lower my head and bring my palms together to begin my prayer. I don't care how many people are watching me as I pray in this parking lot. This quiet time with God before I begin this school day is absolutely necessary.

Dear God, I come to You as humbly as I know and thanking You for another day that I get to spend in Your presence. Thank You for blessing my family and friends with another chance to get closer to You. Thank You for also allowing us to see another year of school. It is my prayer that You bless this school year that is upon us, God. I'm feeling a bit nervous right now, but I pray that You give me the strength, the courage, and the confidence that I need to make it through this year successfully.

In addition, I pray that You watch over my brother and sister while they are here. I hope that my brother enjoys his senior year of high school, and that You protect him when he's out there on the football field. I'm worried about my sister and the way that she is being influenced by the things she sees online and the guys that she spends a lot of her time talking to. I pray that she remembers You in everything that she does, and I pray that anything that is not pleasing to You or coming from You is removed from her life. God, please watch over my best friends Mercy, Ava, and Ryann too this year. I love them so much, and I know that we are all facing different struggles. However, I know Your ways and I know that You've got us covered. Thank You so much! In Jesus' name I pray, amen.

As I lift my head from prayer, I feel this rush of calmness flow through my veins. At this point, I am ready to tackle this school week. It is amazing to see how one prayer has the power to change your entire outlook.

Walking down the halls of KHS, I begin to notice how out of place I am. Walking past the first set of lockers, I see a group of girls whispering to one of her friends about only Lord knows what and pointing at an overweight girl with braces and glasses at the lockers across from them. Further down the hall, I notice this short girl who was in my science class last year in a tiny, red dress boo'd up with this tall guy in a football letterman jacket. Beside them, there is a handsome guy who I remember seeing at my church yesterday. I think his name is Christian or something like that.

I cannot help but to admire this guy's attire. He has on khaki pants with a navy-blue blazer and a red bowtie to match, and it looks amazing on him. He also has the same light brown eyes as me, and he has a warm, caramel skin complexion. He's about 6'6 in height, so I figure he must play basketball because he doesn't look muscular enough to be a football player.

As I prepare to walk past this handsome brother, I speed up and pretend like I'm texting on my phone so he won't say anything to me.

"Well good morning, beautiful," he says.

As I look behind me to make sure that he is in fact talking to me, he says, “Yeah, I’m talking to you. Good morning, Love.” It’s as if he knew I was surprised he was actually speaking to me, and I can feel my cheeks warming up as I smile automatically. I hope I’m not blushing too hard.

“Good morning,” I say, stopping in my place.

Lord, give me strength.

“Do you remember me,” he asks.

“You visited our church, right? Could you remind me of your name again?” I ask. I don’t want to be embarrassed later by calling him Christian if that isn’t his name.

“Sorry, I’m Christian. Christian Carter,” he says, revealing some super cute dimples. I see I was right about the name though.

“Well, it’s nice to meet you again, Christian. I’m Love Hudson.” Given how nervous I am, I’m surprised I didn’t forget my own name.

“Yeah, I know. Your name is as beautiful as you are,” he responds.

Lord, help me. I think he’s flirting, but I don’t even know how to flirt back!

“When I saw you at church I was captured by your beauty. You radiate confidence not only in yourself but in God as well,” Christian says, looking me straight in my eyes. “Plus, when you opened your mouth to sing you took everyone to

Heaven including me. You have the most angelic voice that I have ever heard, Love."

Wow. I'm even more speechless after that. No guy has ever told me anything so sweet. Considering that I don't think I'm confident enough, his compliment resonates deeply within me. His attractiveness makes it even harder for me to maintain my cool, and my shyness begins to overtake me. I need to say something!

After a long pause, I say, "Thanks." I wish I could've said more, but his compliments were so unexpected, especially for our first real conversation. I can't believe he is being so straightforward with me. I wonder if he's like this all the time. He probably tells all of the pretty girls things like this.

"I'm sorry if I caught you off guard," Christian says, basically reading my mind again. "I planned in my head what I would say to you if I ever got the chance to talk to you one-on-one, and that was something I didn't even plan to say." He looks at his feet and rubs the back of his neck. I wonder what he actually planned to say, but I'm too afraid to ask.

Luckily the first bell rings, signaling that it is time to begin heading to our homeroom classrooms. I have to get out of here before I completely lose my composure.

"It's cool." I nervously giggle as I attempt to walk away and head toward Mrs. Ford's classroom.

"Carter and Hudson? Shouldn't we be in the same homeroom? Let's walk together," Christian says before I have a chance to walk away from him. Homerooms are divided up by last names. The letters A through L are in one classroom, and M through Z are in another. I seriously hope I'm not coming off as an awkward, shy girl to him though.

"Yeah, let's go," I respond, running my hands through my fro.

As I do that, I notice Christian smiling and shaking his head at me.

"What?" I ask.

"That fro is so freakin' cute on you."

"Let's get to class before we're late." I say, turning my head in the opposite direction so he won't notice that I'm blushing.

Since I told my sister I would meet her and Ava in class, I wonder what they are going to say when they see me walking into the classroom with Christian by my side. I know we're not a couple or anything, but the fact that I'm actually with a guy like him is a sight to see. If we were to date in the future, I believe we would complement each other well.

As soon as this thought flashes through my head, I remember the conversation that I had with my brother and sister this morning in the car. A boyfriend is the last thing that should be on my mind right now. I have so many other things to worry about, like starting this school year off strong, but I'm more focused on Christian at the moment. It's crazy how I already feel some type of connection with him, and I barely know anything about this guy. I can't put to words what I'm feeling, but it's electrifying and refreshing.

I see a lot of girls eyeing Christian and me as we continue walking down the hallway. I hope they don't think we are together, but then again, I wouldn't mind if they did, considering how attractive he is. Maybe they won't try to hit on him if they assume he's already taken by me. Then I won't have any competition when it comes to him.

When we finally make it to our side of the building, I wonder what he's thinking about. He has been pretty silent since I agreed to walk with him to homeroom, and that's weird considering he had so much to say before. He appears to be in deep thought, but about what though? I wish I was bold enough to ask him what's going on in his head, but I don't know if I should be the one to break the silence.

"What are you over there thinking about?" Christian asks with a smirk on his face. I could have asked him the exact same question.

"Oh, nothing really," I say, wondering if my face looked as dazed as I was feeling. Why am I feeling this guy so much? I need to pray about this before I get too ahead of myself.

"Nothing, huh?" he asks, opening the door to our classroom for me. Well, now I know that he knows a little bit about chivalry. That's another good sign.

Walking into the classroom, I scan the room to see if I can find where Truth and Ava are sitting. There has to be like two hundred people in this room. It reminds me of one of those lecture rooms we saw when we were on a college visit at The University of Arkansas with Micah. I can tell that some of the girls in here are drooling over Christian already, and I notice one girl in the fourth row who rolls her eyes as soon as she notices us together. Yeah, he's definitely a ladies' man.

"Let's sit here." Christian motions toward two empty seats in the second row on the left. They are the only seats that don't seem to be taken.

"Ok," I respond, still looking around for my sister and friend as we head over to claim the two seats. I think Truth and Ava will understand me not sitting with them because it is nearly impossible to find anyone in particular in this large room. Plus, they probably aren't even here yet. Neither of them are very punctual.

As soon as Christian and I sit down, my phone begins to vibrate in my oversized, African themed messenger bag. When I look to see who it is, Truth's name flashes across the lockscreen.

Truth: Girl, who is that????!!!!!!!

Love: Christian Carter. Remember him from church?

Truth: Nah, but he is fine ;)

Love: I agree lol

Truth: Tell him your twin said what's up

Love: Girl bye lol...He doesn't wanna talk to you hahahaha

Truth: Whatever! If he has a bro, lemme know <3

Love: Blah. Where are you sitting?

Truth: In the back lol...All the fine guys are back here minus one

Love: Why am I not surprised? #BoyCrazy

Truth: Nah, boys are crazy about Truth #TruthHurts

As I place my phone back in my bag, I notice that Christian is staring at me once again. “What?” I ask him. He has a serious staring problem. It’s cute, but it’s making me uncomfortable.

“Someone is really blowing up your phone this morning.” Christian laughs. “I bet you have all the guys in this school hitting you up.” If only he knew how untrue that was. My phone stays desert dry.

“No, it’s just my twin,” I respond, looking behind me to see if I can spot her in this crowded room.

“You have a twin?” He looks amused.

“Yes. She’s basically me without the fro. Didn’t you see her at church?”

“Nope. I guess I was too focused on you,” Christian responds, showing off his perfect smile again. Once again, I don’t know what to say to him, so I just smile and shake my head.

After a couple of minutes pass, he asks, “So, is your twin anything like you?”

“Umm, if you’re asking does she look like me, then yes.”

"Ha! I see you have a sense of humor, but you know that's not what I meant, Love."

"I know," I say, laughing. "We have a few things in common, but for the most part we're totally different."

"Interesting. I have a twin too," Christian says.

"You're lying!"

"I'm not lying. His name is Nehemiah," he replies with a serious look on his face.

"How come I've never seen him before then? Was he at church?"

"Well, long story short, he wasn't here last year, and no he wasn't at church either," he says, glancing at his feet.

"Why not?" I ask.

"My parents divorced last year right before the end of summer. It was a nasty divorce, and they thought it would be a good idea to split us up," he reveals. I can feel the pain resonating from his voice.

I can't imagine living without my twin for a day, so I can only imagine what Christian and his brother went through. I don't understand how his parents thought it was a good idea to split up two brothers like that, especially at their age.

Without thinking, I grasp his hands and say, "Wow, I'm so sorry to hear that. How did you guys deal with it?"

"It was hard, Love. I'm not even gonna lie. My bro is my best friend. Having him all the way in Cali with my mom while I was here in Georgia with my father was tough. I'm so glad he's back," he says, glancing across the room. "He's sitting over there." With one hand still holding onto mine, Christian points to the other side of the room with his free hand and I spot his brother.

Nehemiah looks exactly like Christian. Even though he's sitting, I can tell that he is just as tall, if not taller, than Christian. He's wearing a black t-shirt with the words "God First Bro" written across the front in big, white letters. Nice choice.

"You guys look exactly alike," I say in disbelief.

"Duh, we're twins," he sarcastically responds before laughing and flashing his dimples once more.

"Now who's being funny?" I release Christian's hand to pick up my phone to text my sister about this newfound discovery of mine.

Love: He has a twin too!

Truth: Is he in here?

Love: Yeah, front row w/ black shirt.

Truth: Right or left?

Love: Right.

Truth: It's lit!

Finally, Mrs. Ford walks in the classroom. I didn't even notice that she wasn't here. It feels like we've already been in here for 10 minutes, but I'm not going to complain. I'm really enjoying being in Christian's presence and getting to know him a little better. It usually takes me a while before I'm totally myself around a person, but I don't see anything wrong with me letting my guard down with him just a little bit. So far, he seems like a good guy, but only time will tell. This new year has already brought new beginnings, and I'm excited to see where all of this goes.

~2~

Girl in Charge

"If you fail under pressure, your strength is too small."
Proverbs 24:10 NLT

Mercy
As I attempt to sneak into Miss Mason's homeroom classroom seven minutes late, I laugh to myself. I can't believe this is how I'm beginning the first day of my sophomore year. I don't regret being late though. Things with Joel got a little spicy as we were on our way to school.

Joel Jackson, a senior here at KHS, has been my boyfriend for almost a year now. We met last year when I was at cheer practice. I was doing my thing on the sidelines of the football field while he was practicing with the football team. I noticed him checking me out, and after practice he chased me down as I was about to head out with my girls. Little did I know, he was the star wide receiver of the KHS Panthers. He's also best friends with Micah, Love and Truth's older brother, so I figured he must be a good guy.

Our relationship hasn't been all peaches and cream though. A lot of people were saying mean things about me because I was a freshman dating an upperclassman. If I had a dollar for every time someone called me "loose" or a "fast lil girl", I'd be a billionaire by now. Everyone was trying to convince me that Joel was just using me for sex, including my dad, who is a deacon at Trinity Christian Center.

It was so stressful to hear so many negative things like that about the guy I loved, and I had to quickly grow some tough skin. Despite the rumors, I knew the truth and didn't let that change the way I felt about my boyfriend. Joel was nothing like the person everyone was trying to make him out to be. Now, we are the power couple of KHS, and everyone loves us. Well, almost everyone.

"Miss Perez, it's nice that you could finally join us," Miss Mason says as I enter her classroom. "Now take a seat, so I can continue with the announcements as I was doing before you graced us with your presence." I heard through my mom, Dr. Rina Perez, who is the AP Physics teacher here, that Miss Mason is recently divorced but I didn't think her attitude would be this rude.

"Sorry, Miss Mason. I was having a bit of car trouble this morning, and it won't happen again," I lie with the most innocent face I could conjure up. I didn't even drive to school.

Joel picked me up from my house in his new Dodge Challenger, which was an early birthday gift from his parents. We would've been on time if we didn't chill in the driveway for so long. We hadn't seen each other in three whole days, so I think being a little late for school was acceptable.

"I didn't ask you all of that. I said take a seat." Miss Mason rolls her eyes.

"Yes ma'am." I smile. I have a reputation to uphold, so I can't let this old lady get to me this morning. I'm the new and youngest cheer captain ever for Panther Cheer, and I am also class president. Plus, my part-time job consists of keeping the haters mad.

Hopefully, Miss Mason doesn't run and tell my mom that I was late making it to her class this morning because I know the teachers at this school like to run their mouths. My mom would throw a hissy fit if she knew me and Joel arrived late.

It's so hard trying to find a seat in here because there are too many students in this lecture hall. Ryann is in this homeroom, so I look around to see if I can find out where she's sitting. Luckily, I spot her pale, white skin and bright red hair at the end of the third row.

"Hey love," I say, strutting over to take a seat. All eyes are still on me, so I flip my long curls over my shoulder like the diva that I am.

"What's up, girl? What took you so long to get here? I know your brand-new Jaguar isn't messing up already," Ryann asks. She's right though. I just got a new Jaguar for my 16th birthday, and it better not have any problems anytime soon. Otherwise, my daddy will be buying me a new one.

"Well, let's just say Joel and I had an amazing morning," I reveal, winking my eye at her.

"Hold up! I thought you weren't giving up the goods yet," she says, moving in closer to me.

"I'm not," I reply with a huge smirk on my face.

"You might as well go ahead and do it. Everyone already thinks y'all have gone all the way anyways," Ryann responds. I'm well aware of what people think about Joel and me, but I don't care. I'm not doing anything that I know I'm not ready for. These people need to find relationships of their own to worry about and keep their mouths off of me and Joel's relationship.

"A girl who doesn't stand for something will fall for anything. Wise words from Pastor Hudson." I enlighten Ryann on what the twins' father preached about this Sunday. I know it may be hard to believe sometimes, but I am a Christian. I'm not a perfect angel because I like to have fun and enjoy life too, but God is working on me.

"Whatever girl. Don't start talking all godly on me this morning," Ryann says, which reminds me that she is an atheist.

Miss Mason begins to call attendance, and my phone vibrates. I look at the screen, and it's Joel.

Joel: You're in Miss Mason's class?

Mercy: Unfortunately.

Joel: I'm walking you to your next class.

Mercy: Babe, you might be late. My next class is on the far side of the school.

Joel: Don't you know who I am?

Mercy: Lol what is that supposed to mean?

Joel: I'm Joel Jackson, and I do what I want. They love me here lol

Mercy: Cocky much? Lol

*Joel: You love it though :-**

Mercy: Si ;)

Joel: Yep. I'll see you in a few minutes boo. Love you!

Mercy: Who loves me?

Joel: Joel loves you ;)

Mercy: That's better :)

I didn't even tell him that I love him back, but he'll be alright. I think I told him enough this morning to last him a lifetime. That's my baby.

Catching me off guard, Miss Mason yells, "Miss Perez?!"

"Yes ma'am?"

"It would be nice if you could put your phone down for a second and answer for roll call," she responds.

"Sorry, it was really important. I'll pay more attention next time." I flash my biggest smile at her yet again. This lady must really hate me. I haven't heard her say one word to another student in here. She needs to chill. Plus, she already knew I was here anyways.

As Miss Mason turns her attention away from me to proceed with roll call, I nudge Ryann in the arm. "Why didn't you tell me she was calling my name?"

"I didn't even know she was calling you. After she called my name, I tuned her out," Ryann says.

Noticing this strange look on her face that wasn't there before, I ask, "What's going on in your head, Ryann?"

"I'm just thinking about some things."

"Things like what?" I ask, sensing something is wrong with her.

"It's just stuff at home. Things are crazy right now, and I don't know what to do. Please don't say just pray either because I'm not trying to hear it this morning."

"That's not what I was going to say," I lie. "Talk to me. I'm all ears."

"I really don't wanna talk about it, but I'm tired of holding all this stuff in. My family is too broke to function, and I need to get a job to help my mom out."

"What are you going to do about basketball though?"

"That's what I'm trying to figure out. I know I was born to ball, and I know that's probably one of the only ways that I'll get a full-ride scholarship to college since my grades aren't good."

"Don't worry, boo. It's all going to work out somehow. I just know it will," I say.

Ryann is an amazing basketball player. Honestly, I've never seen a player like her, male or female. She averaged 25 points per game last year, and she won Rookie of the Year for KHS's varsity girls' basketball team. She was the only freshman allowed to play on the team because she was so good. She was also a major key in the girls' basketball team winning their first state championship in school history. That's why I hate seeing her go through all of this. She has a bright future ahead of herself, but life keeps getting in the way of everything.

Ryann's father left her, her mother, and her older brother behind when she was only three years old. Now her mom has four kids, Ryann, Romeo, Reagan, and River. Romeo is a junior at KHS, Reagan is a freshman, and River is in the fourth grade, and she's working two different jobs and is hardly ever home. She has had it bad for a while now, and things don't seem to be getting any better for them.

"I just don't know how much more I can take. I'm too young to be going through all of this," Ryann says with tears forming in her eyes.

"I know how you feel. We all have to go through storms in life in order to appreciate the sunshine. You know what I mean?"

"Yeah, I see what you mean. It just feels like my whole life has been one big storm with nothing but clouds in sight."

"It can't rain forever." I can see the pain behind her eyes, but beyond all of that pain I sense a glimmer of hope.

"Te amo, chica." Ryann wipes her tears as a soft smile begins to form on her face.

"I love you more."

Just when I say that, the bell begins to ring, which signals that it is time to go to our first period classrooms. As I head to the door, I begin to hear a lot of commotion outside in the hallway. I wonder what's going on. It's too early in the day for there to already be a fight going on, but I wouldn't be surprised if there was one happening right now.

"Girl, look!" Ryann stops in the center of the doorway.

"Oh my God! Joel!" I yell.

Joel is standing in the middle of a heart created through the use of pink and red rose petals and small, white candles. Behind him, some of his football friends are standing and holding up various posters saying, "I love you Mercy", "Be Mine", and "Can I have Mercy?"

"Babe?" Joel says, grabbing my hand and looking me directly in my gray eyes.

"Yes?" I ask. This whole thing feels like something you would only see in movies. "What's going on, Joel?"

"Mercy, you know I love you, right?" he asks, beginning to get down on one knee.

After I don't respond for a minute, Joel says, "Um, Mercy? You know I love you, right?" I didn't even realize I had zoned out.

"Lo siento. Yes, I know you love me. I love you more." I look down at him as he reaches in the pocket of his KHS football letterman jacket.

"Not even possible," Joel replies, pulling a small, black box out of his pocket. "Will you promise me something though, Mercy?"

"Promise you what, Joel?"

"Promise me that you'll always love me. Promise me that you're in this for the long haul."

"I promise." I look from his eyes to the small box and then back to his eyes. He's literally crying right now. This is the first time I've ever seen him cry.

Finally opening the black box and revealing a small ring with a heart shaped centerpiece and a beautiful diamond in the center of the heart, Joel continues, "Will you accept a promise from me?"

With tears forming in my own eyes, I respond, "I will."

If there is such a thing as a completely perfect moment, it would be what I am experiencing right now. I can't imagine anything more beautiful than this, and the fact that this is coming from the guy that I love so much makes this moment even more beautiful.

"I promise to stick by you when things get rough. I promise to always make you a priority. I promise to never make you forget how much I love you. I promise you I'm in this for the long haul too. Mercy Perez, I love you. I promise I always will. Accept this promise ring from me to remind you of the promises I just made to you today," he says, placing the promise ring on the ring finger of my left hand.

"Gracias," I respond, tears rolling down my face at this point. The ring is a perfect fit. I can't hold all of my emotions in, so I embrace Joel's 6'2 frame in a tight hug as I begin to bawl.

"Dang baby!" Joel says. "I do have a game to play in on Friday."

"Sorry, I didn't mean to hurt you," I say, loosening my grip on him.

"There's more," Joel whispers in my ear.

"More?" I ask, still crying and holding onto him.

"I know it's a lil early, but will you be my date to homecoming? This is my last one, so it would mean a lot to me if you went with me, Mercy. How does that sound to you?" he asks, cupping my face with his large hands and kissing my tears away.

"Yes! Yes, Joel! I'd love to go to homecoming with you again," I reply, reaching in to kiss my man.

The rest of the students in the hallway begin clapping, and I can't help but feel like the luckiest girl on earth right now. It's every girl's dream to go to homecoming with an upperclassman, and I have the best one of them all. What a great way to start my sophomore year of high school!

Moments later, I hear "Ew! Stop all of that!" as my sister, Joy, interrupts me and Joel's public display of affection. Joy is a senior here at KHS. She was also friends with Joel before we started dating because they went to junior high school together. She is also dating Micah.

"Hello to you, too," I reply, slightly annoyed that she just interrupted the moment I was having.

"Congrats on the homecoming proposal," Joy says as the crowd begins to disperse.

"Thanks! Micah might need to take notes," I joke.

"Micah taught Joel all that he knows. Don't play," she replies with mock seriousness in her voice as she reaches in to hug me. She's probably right though. Micah is a great boyfriend to her, and I know he respects her out of the respect that he has for God. That is something special and rare to find in our generation.

"I think it's the other way around. I put Micah up on all the game when he made it to ATL," Joel says, reaching to hug Joy.

"Boy whatever. Just treat my sister right, and we won't have any problems," Joy replies, hugging Joel in return.

"You don't have to worry about that." Joel kisses my forehead.

"You sure don't," Micah says, seemingly coming out of nowhere. "How are you beautiful ladies this morning?"

"I'm doing well. Good morning, mi amor," Joy says, looking Micah in the eyes. Anyone can tell that she's deeply in love with him, and I love seeing her this happy.

"I'm doing even better now thanks to Joel," I reply.

"God bless y'all. Joy and I are about to head to class. We'll see y'all later. Congrats, lil sis," Micah says, wrapping me up in a hug.

"Thanks, brother. God bless you too," I respond. He's like the big brother I never had, and he's always looking out for me and my sister.

As I watch Micah and Joy walk away, I remember that I do have a class I need to get to. I already made one bad impression on a teacher, and I don't need to make another one on the first day back.

Reaching for Joel's hand, I say, "Babe, we should probably head to class if we want to be on time."

"Let's go then, shawty," he responds, sounding like a true Southern boy.

Walking down the hall with Joel always makes me feel proud. Knowing that we're such a beautiful, powerful couple, it's no wonder that we're the most talked about couple at KHS. I'm the queen here, and he's my king.

As Joel and I begin walking down the stairs to the second floor of the school, we walk past his ex-girlfriend, Mercury. Her mouth drops wide open as if she's surprised to see us together or something. It's obvious that I'm an upgrade from a girl like her. She caused so much drama in the beginning of our relationship because she was still so obsessed with Joel after their breakup, and he obviously wanted someone better. The breakup must've hit her hard because she's looking like a bum, considering that it's the first day of school and she's dressed in sweats. She clearly picked up a lot of weight over the summer, and her weave is looking a mess.

"Good morning, Mercury," I say, being petty.

"Good morning to you, too," she replies, stopping in the middle of the staircase. I guess she's feeling a little bold this morning, and so am I.

"What's up with you?" I look her up and down, but she doesn't appear to be rattled.

"Maybe you should ask your boyfriend what's up with me. Now have a good day, sweetheart." Mercury grins as she walks away leaving me speechless. What the heck is that supposed to mean? Ask your boyfriend?

"Joel, what is she talking about?" I glare at him.

"Mercy, just ignore her. She's just trying to make you mad like you were trying to make her mad too. Don't start this school year with drama, girl."

"Girl? Who do you think you're talking to, Joel?" I raise my voice. He doesn't even seem to be fazed by Mercury's remarks.

"You need to chill before you cause a scene. Why are you trying to ruin our perfect morning?" he replies, kissing me and reminding me of how I felt before this encounter with Mercury happened.

"Whatever." I sigh, snatching away from him.

"Don't be like that, Mercy." Joel hugs me from behind. He knows my weakness.

"Look, Joel. Can we just get to class?" I ask, folding my arms across my small chest.

"That's what I thought we were doing. Come on," he replies, suddenly lifting me off of my feet to carry me.

He's doing the most right now, but he better not be keeping any secrets from me. It's not going to be pretty if I find out that there's more to what Mercury just said. Nothing goes hidden at KHS anyways.

The rest of the first day back at school was uneventful, and now I'm getting ready for the first cheerleading practice of the season. I'm a little nervous because this is my first time leading practice as captain. I have a lot of exciting things planned for this season, and I can't wait to begin working on everything. Plus, I have my chicas Love and Truth right along with me, and the weather is perfect today. It's a nice, sunny, 80-degree day with a slight breeze.

We have 20 girls on the squad this year. Two of the girls are freshmen, ten are sophomores, four are juniors, and four are seniors. Unfortunately, two of the senior girls, Makayla and Ashley, are friends with Mercury. It's going to be interesting to see how well we get along this year with me being captain. I don't plan on taking any mess from them or anyone else on the team. Anybody who can't understand that, can get off of my team.

Dear Heavenly Father, thank You for always being with me and for putting me in a position of leadership. I pray that You forgive me for all the sinning that I've done today, and I pray that You just continue to work on me. Lord, I pray for protection over my team this year. I pray that each girl performs to the best of her ability, not only at games but at practice as well. I also pray that we have no unnecessary drama this year. In Jesus' name, amen.

"Circle up, girls!" I yell after finishing my prayer. It's a little noisy around this football field, and I want to make sure everyone hears me. "We're going to begin with stretching as a team, and as we stretch I want everyone to go around the circle and say her name and a fun fact about herself."

"Let me start," Truth says.

"Fine," I say, taking my place in the circle.

"My name is Truth, and I'm a sophomore. This girl to my left is my twin, and we have a brother over there practicing on the field," she says, motioning toward the center of the football field while the rest of our squad giggles.

"Don't y'all ladies stare too much. He's happily taken by my sister, Joy," I let the girls know before any of them tried anything sneaky.

"What she said!" Truth says. "You're next, Love."

"Well, I'm Love. I'm a sophomore, and I love singing, reading, and cheering," Love introduces herself.

"What else do you love?" I ask, knowing that she's forgetting the most important thing about her.

"Oh! I luhhh God," Love adds, flashing a big smile as the team giggles again. That's my girl. I admire her relationship with God so much. She has such a boldness about her love for Him, and I wish I had that type of boldness.

"Thank you," I say, winking at Love. "I'm Mercy Perez, and I'm captain of the squad this year. I'm a sophomore, and I love shopping and socializing. I'm also excited for all of the great things that I know we're going to accomplish as a team this year."

"You're forgetting something, girl. What else do you love, or rather who do you love?" Truth interrupts.

"Oh! How could I forget? I love, love, love Joel Jackson," I say, sounding like the proud girlfriend that I am.

However, I notice Mercury's friends rolling their eyes at me. Dang, are they feeling salty already?

As the remaining girls go around the circle and tell a little bit about themselves, I become even more excited. We are a team of phenomenal girls, and it is such a blessing to be able to lead them this year. Unfortunately, but not to my surprise, when it is time for Makayla and Ashley to introduce themselves, I sense some tension from them once again.

"So, I'm Makayla. This is my fourth year on the team, and I plan to go out with a bang. My best friends are Ashley and this former cheerleader named Mercury. It's too bad, well maybe not so bad for some people on this team, that Mercury won't be joining us this year," Makayla says.

What the heck is up with that comment "not so bad for some people on this team" though? She's doing too much, and I don't care how much "seniority" she thinks she has on this team. I will have her put off if she doesn't stop with the mess.

I don't have a clue as to why Mercury decided not to be on the team this year. I assumed that it was because I was voted in as captain for this year over her, but maybe there is more to the story. Maybe she's embarrassed about all that weight that she has picked up over the summer and is afraid to publicly show herself off in a uniform looking like that. I don't mean to be judgmental, but I'm just being honest.

Lord, forgive me.

Interrupting my internal criticism of her best friend, Ashley says, "Hi, my name is Ashley. I'm also a senior on the team, and I would have been more excited to cheer this season if our girl Mercury was still on the team. She was the best captain ever. No shade towards Mercy though."

"It'll take a lot more than that to shade me," I respond, wanting to smack that little smirk off of her face.

At the perfect time, our cheer coach, Coach Goodwin, finally makes her way over to us and says, "Good evening, girls! I'm so happy to see all of you again, and I look forward to another great season. First, I will be assigning y'all to stunt groups."

I'm a flyer, and I'm curious about who I will be stunting with this year. Last year, both of my bases were seniors. My backspot was Jael, though, who is also a sophomore.

"Alright, so our first stunt group will be Mercy's stunt group. Let me get Jael at backspot," Coach Goodwin says, much to my pleasure. "Makayla and Ashley, you girls will be the bases." Coach Goodwin has to be out of her mind. I'm not letting those girls put me in the air. They don't like me, and I don't like them either.

"Is there a problem?" Coach Goodwin asks, noticing the displeasure clearly written on my face.

As I look at Makayla and Ashley, I notice them and their sneaky smiles, but I quickly reply, "No ma'am. There's no problem at all."

I was thinking about telling Coach how much drama Makayla and Ashley have been causing in my life for the past year, but I don't do it despite how badly I want to. I'm the captain AKA the girl in charge, so I just have to suck it up and lead the best way that I know how. Makayla and Ashley want to see me crack under pressure, but I won't give them the pleasure of seeing me do so. However, I don't trust them as high as they can throw me, so this will be interesting.

~3~

Uncertain

"I came to you in weakness—timid and trembling."

1 Corinthians 2:3 NLT

Truth

Now that school and practice are over, maybe I can get started on my homework. Last year, I didn't try as hard on my school work as I could have. I was more focused on cheering, partying, looking good, and getting guys. I'm not saying that I'm taking my focus off of these things, but I do want to work harder in school. Love and Micah do well in school, and it's time for me to do the same.

Mercy agreed to come over to help me study. I could've asked my sister, but I needed to talk to Mercy about what happened while my family was on vacation.

"Girl, guess what," I say, walking into my room and throwing my bag on my bed.

"Girl, what?" Mercy says, taking a seat at my desk on the other side of my room.

"When we were in Florida, I met Young Rue," I say. Young Rue is one of the hottest rappers out in Atlanta right now. He's 18, fine as heck, tatted up, and rich, and I just happened to bump into him at a club in Florida. I know I wasn't supposed to be there, but that's not the point.

"You're lying!"

"I'm dead serious."

"How did you meet him? Was he in concert?" Mercy asks, heading over to take a seat beside me on the bed.

"No, we met at a club." I'm not afraid to tell Mercy about me sneaking out to a club because I know she won't go running her mouth about it. I would've told Love, but she would've been mad about me sneaking out, and she might've snitched to Micah.

"A club? Girl, you are wild!" Mercy says. "How did it happen? Tell me everything."

Moving in closer to Mercy, I say, "I was taking a walk on the beach because I needed to clear my head. Then, I ran into a group of drunk girls who were probably only a few years older than us. They asked me if I wanted to join them, and I said yeah."

"You were drinking?" Mercy asks, practically screaming.

"Shhh, girl! I don't want my folk hearing us, and no I wasn't drinking. I was just with them."

"Oh, sorry. Continue please," Mercy says, lowering her voice.

As soon as Mercy is quiet, I continue, "Well, we ended up in this club, and—"

Interrupting me again, Mercy asks, "How did they even let you in? You're only 15."

"Girl, can I finish the story or not? They weren't even ID'ing people, so I got in easily," I reply, eager to get to the part about Young Rue.

"Sorry, sorry! Go ahead."

"After we got in, we were just dancing for a while. Then, I took a seat at the bar for a little while because I didn't want to completely sweat my edges out. I literally wasn't sitting there for two minutes before I saw him."

Interrupting me yet again, Mercy asks, "Saw who? Rue?"

"Yeah! Who else would I be talking about?"

"I'm just making sure. I'm not going to say anything else." Mercy pretends to zip her lips.

"Good. I didn't know for sure if that was him until I felt someone tap on my shoulder at the bar, and it was him. He was standing there staring at me, and I was speechless."

"What did he say to you?"

Remembering the night very clearly, I say, "He was like 'Baby, why you stop dancing? I was watching you the whole time.' He was looking so good, and I literally wanted to twerk on him as soon as he said that."

"I know I would have!" Mercy laughs. "What happened after that?"

"We danced, chilled in the VIP section, and left."

Visibly shocked, Mercy asks, "Y'all left together?"

"Yeah, we did. He drove us back to his beach house, and we just chilled on the balcony and talked until sunrise. Then, I told him I needed to head home, and he drove me back," I say, reminiscing. "He gave me his number too."

"Did you text him?"

As soon as Mercy asks me that, my bedroom door opens and it's Love. I hope she didn't overhear anything.

"Text who?" Love asks, walking over to take a seat in the bean bag chair by the window. I thought about telling her about the Young Rue encounter, but leaving out the details of me sneaking out. I don't like keeping things from Love, but I don't want her trying to talk me out of getting involved with him because he's a rapper.

Looking from Mercy to Love to back to Mercy, I sigh and reluctantly confess, "Young Rue."

"Young Rue?" Love asks, seemingly confused. I doubt she has ever heard his music. His name has been ringing a lot throughout Atlanta though, so I don't know how she doesn't recognize the name.

Glaring at Love, Mercy says, "The rapper! You don't know who he is?"

"Oh, I knew that name sounded familiar," Love responds. "How did you get his number?"

After a long pause, I reply, "In Florida."

"That night you snuck out, huh?" Love asks, surprising the heck out of me.

How does she even know about that? She must've heard me and Mercy talking before she came in. That's the only way she could've known because no one even knew that I left the resort when we were in Florida.

"Truth, we're twins. Sometimes I just sense things even when you don't tell me. Stop thinking you have to hide everything from me." I feel bad for keeping this from her now. I don't know why, but I feel like I have to keep a lot of things from Love. She's so sweet and innocent, and I know I'm not, and it bothers me sometimes.

"My bad, Love. I just didn't want you judging me or running to tell Micah," I admit.

"Truth, really? You know me better than that. Have I ever judged you or ran and told Micah something that you didn't want me to?" Love asks and I shake my head "no." I don't even know why I'm tripping.

After a few moments pass by, Mercy asks again, “So, have you texted him?”

I respond, “No.”

“Why not?” Mercy asks. Most girls would jump on the opportunity to text or call Young Rue, but I haven’t. It’s because I don’t know what to say to him, and I also don’t want to have to tell him that I’m only 15. It might turn him away, and I don’t want to blow this. I’d love to be known as Young Rue’s girl, but I wish that I was like two or three years older.

“Should I text him?” I ask, looking at both Mercy and my sister. I know Mercy is going to say yes, but I can bet a dollar that Love says no.

To my surprise, Mercy and Love both say, “Yes.”

“Hold up!” I shout, looking past Mercy to glance at Love. “Love, what did you just say?” I can’t believe she just said yes. She must be feeling sick today or something.

“You heard me. Go for it. I know you’re going to do what you want to do regardless of what we say,” Love responds. My sister knows how headstrong I am, and once I have my mind set on something, I go after it by any means necessary.

“Ok, I’m about to do it,” I nervously say, picking up my cell phone. “I’m going to do it right now.”

Truth: Hey, it’s Truth.

After I press send, I place my phone on my bedside table and sit quietly. I'm scared he won't respond, or worse, he won't remember me.

Breaking the silence, Love asks, "So now what?"

Glancing at my clock which reads 6:01 p.m., Mercy replies, "We wait," and that's exactly what we do. We wait and wait and wait for what seems like forever, but only ten minutes have passed.

Once I'm tired of waiting, I say, "Let's get started on our homework."

I don't know if Young Rue is going to text back, but I don't want to be looking like a fool by sitting around waiting on him. I'm usually the one making guys wait, so this is new territory for me. I'm uncertain about how this is going to turn out. Either way it goes, this homework isn't going to do itself.

***

Despite how busy this week has been, I still can't get Young Rue off of my mind. It has been two whole days since I sent that text to him, and he still hasn't responded. I've been getting texts from the finest guys at KHS, but none of that matters right now. I'm not even going to lie and say that I'm not disappointed because I am. I felt like Rue was feeling me back in Florida, but I guess I was wrong.

As I head toward the table that I'm sharing with my girls minus Love with my lunch tray filled with mystery meat and green stuff, I realize how ready I am for this week to be over. I just need some time to myself because I'm letting this Rue situation get to me a little too much. Maybe I should have joined Love in the library so I can get my mind focused on something else.

As soon as I sit down in my chair next to Ava, she asks, "What wrong, boo? You upset?" with her not-so-perfect English. She and her family moved to the United States from South Korea when we were in the eighth grade, and we've been tight ever since. Aside from my sister, Ava is always one of the first ones to notice when I'm having a bad day. I can't fake anything around her.

"Nah, I'm good," I lie. I haven't told Ava and Ryann about Young Rue yet, and I don't want to mention it to them right now.

"Ok, sure," Ava responds, giving me the eye like she knows that something is up with me that I'm not telling her. "Mrs. Dee said she want to meet with you after lunch."

"Meet with me?" I ask.

"Yeah you," Ava says.

"Meet with me for what?" Mrs. Dee is one of the coolest people at KHS. She's the guidance counselor, and she gives some of the best advice. I used to sneak to her office whenever I would get kicked out of class for my smart mouth.

"How I supposed to know?" Ava says. "She only told me to tell you."

"Why were you talking to Mrs. Dee?" Mercy asks Ava.

"I work in the main office now," Ava responds.

"I didn't know that," Ryann says. "When did you start?"

"Now you know," Ava responds, sassily. "I started today. You want a job too?"

"Does it pay?" Ryann asks.

"I wish," Ava says. "Then, I wouldn't have to ask Dad for nothing." Ava's dad is the CEO of this huge company in downtown Atlanta, while her mom is a stay-at-home mom. Her dad brings in a lot of bread, but he's really hard on Ava. He expects her to go into corporate America in the future, but she has dreams of being a professional dancer.

"You know I don't mind asking my daddy for anything," Mercy says. She's so spoiled. "I'm going to use his money as long as he's making it."

"Lucky you," Ryann says, dejectedly. She's acting like something is wrong with her today, but I'll see what's up with her later.

"I guess I'll go ahead and see what Mrs. Dee wants," I say, getting up to return my tray. "I'll catch up with y'all after school."

The walk to Mrs. Dee's office takes about five minutes because the cafeteria is in a separate building. There are so many students outside in the courtyard just chilling and enjoying this little break from class. Usually I would take my time strolling through here, but I really want to see why Mrs. Dee needs to see me.

When I make it to her office, I notice a large vase of a dozen red roses sitting at the front of her desk. They're probably from her husband. She just recently married a retired professional football player, and he's so fine.

"Good afternoon, Truth?" Mrs. Dee asks, walking to take a seat behind her desk. "How are you?"

"I'm doing good. How you doing?"

"Everything is going well on my end. I see Ava relayed my message to you."

"Yeah, she did. What did I do this time?"

"You didn't do anything as far as I know." Mrs. Dee laughs. "I just wanted to talk to you about a few things."

"A few things like what?"

"Your grades," Mrs. Dee says, pulling up a file on her computer.

"We don't even have any grades yet," I say, hoping that I didn't accidentally forget to turn something in.

"I'm talking about your grades from last year," Mrs. Dee responds.

"What's wrong with them? I didn't do that bad," I say, scratching my head.

"I know your grades weren't bad at all, but I know that you're capable of so much more, Truth. Am I right?"

After taking a moment to think about what she said, I reply, "Yeah, you're right."

"I thought so. That's why I'm enrolling you in all advanced placement courses. I know you'll do just fine."

"You're joking, right?" I say, rising to my feet. There's no way I'm about to be taking classes with all of those nerds and social rejects just because Mrs. Dee expects more out of me. She must've lost her mind.

"No, I'm serious," Mrs. Dee says, motioning for me to sit back down. "You ended last semester with 5 B's and 2 C's. Your transcript follows you throughout the rest of high school, and you'll have to send it to colleges once you start applying. Colleges take into account the difficulty of your coursework."

"And what is that supposed to mean to me?"

"That means that you need to challenge yourself and push yourself a little harder if you want to get into a good school."

"You must think I'm Love or something?" I ask, rolling my eyes.

"No, Truth. You're a smart girl, and I know what you're capable of. I'm changing your class schedule, and you'll thank me for it later."

"Whatever," I mutter under my breath. I'm so over this right now. "When I flunk, I'm blaming it on you, Mrs. Dee."

"You won't fail. Have a little more faith in yourself, Truth. Believe in yourself like I believe in you," Mrs. Dee says, handing me my new class schedule.

Taking the schedule out of her hand, I ask, "Is that all you wanted?"

"Yes, that's all for now. Enjoy the rest of your day." Mrs. Dee smiles.

"You too," I respond before exiting Mrs. Dee's office and slamming the door on my way out.

Normally I would be sitting in regular Physical Science class, but right now I'm sitting in AP Physics thanks to Mrs. Dee. There are only 9 other students in here, so I can't even pretend to be paying attention without being called out on it. The teacher is Mercy's mother, which is probably a good thing.

Interrupting my thoughts, this white dude in the front looks back at me and says, "How does it feel being the only black kid in here?" Honestly, I didn't even notice that I was the only black student in here. There are three white boys, one white girl, three Asian boys, two Asian girls, and then there's me the black girl.

"How do you think it'll feel when I knock those glasses off of you, Peter?" I respond. I don't even know his name, so I gave him a stereotypical white boy name. This is the first time that I've ever had to deal with someone questioning me because of my blackness, and I don't know how to feel other than pissed off.

"You better leave her alone, man. That's Micah Hudson's sister," the other white boy in front says.

"Listen to your friend," I respond.

I know Micah can handle this little dude, but I don't mind fighting a dude for my respect. These people in here obviously don't know me. I used to get in trouble a lot when I was younger for fighting, but I gave that up once I got to high school. However, I don't mind bringing out the old me if necessary.

"Sorry, I late," someone says walking into the classroom five minutes after the bell has rung and taking a seat next to me. To my surprise, it's Ava.

"It's fine," Dr. Perez says. "Prepare to take notes once I get my PowerPoint slideshow pulled up."

"I didn't know you were taking AP Physics," I say to Ava. I'm glad to have at least someone that I know in this class with me.

"My dad made me," Ava says. "When I make F he going to complain."

"Girl, you're not gonna make an F in this class." I laugh.

"Watch and see," Ava responds, laughing too. "I hate the dude in front."

"Who? Peter?" I say, pointing to the guy who made that racist comment a few minutes ago.

"His name not Peter. It James."

"Close enough," I respond. "This dude had the nerve to ask me how it feels being the only black kid up in here."

"You serious?"

"Yeah I'm serious."

"Want me to knock him out?"

"Nah, girl." I laugh out loud. "You don't have to do that. I'll handle him. Why don't you like him anyways?"

"He think he so smart, and he talk about my dad and his company. He think his dad company better than my dad company."

"Forget dude," I say.

"He a nobody," Ava responds. "Already forgot him."

Just as I start laughing, Dr. Perez goes up to the board and begins teaching. This is going to be a long year of struggle bussing it in Physics.

After school and practice end, my girls and I all come over to my house to eat and chill out before it's time to go to church. Everyone is here but Mercy though. She's probably somewhere drooling behind Joel.

"So how is school going?" Mama asks as she begins preparing dinner.

"Everything is going smoothly for me," Love answers. "I'm enjoying all of my classes."

"That's great, baby," Mama responds. "What about you, Truth?"

"I hate it. I forgot to tell you I'm taking all AP classes now."

"Since when?" Ryann asks.

"Since Mrs. Dee changed my schedule," I respond. They're all looking surprised. "Is it really that big of a deal?"

"I'm glad you're beginning to challenge yourself," Mama says. "How are the classes going so far?"

"She changed my schedule today, so the only AP class I went to today was Physics."

"You're taking AP Physics?" Love asked. "I was scared to take that myself."

"Girl, yeah I'm taking it," I respond.

"I'm taking it too," Ava says. "Tell your mom what James said." I knew Ava was going to bring this up, and I know talking about it is going to get me pissed off all over again.

"Who is James?" Mama asks.

"This white dude in my Physics class," I say, not really wanting to talk about this.

"What about him?"

After I don't say anything right away, Ava says, "He ask Truth how it feel to be the only Black person in there."

"You've got to be kidding me," Ryann says. "I'll fight him."

"Same thing I said!" Ava says.

"It's really not that serious y'all." I roll my eyes.

"James? James Fitzpatrick?" Love asks.

"John Fitzpatrick's boy?" Mama asks.

"Yeah! That's his dad name," Ava answers.

"Don't pay that boy any mind," Mama says. "His father gave me problems when I was in law school."

"Problems how?" I ask. My mama makes everything look so easy, so it's always interesting to hear her talk about problems she had in the past.

"When I was at law school at Harvard, John asked me how I got in. Then, he basically proceeded to argue that I didn't belong there as a woman, a Black woman at that."

"I can see why his son is so racist now," Love responds. "James kept telling one of my teachers last year that my hair was in his way. One day he even touched it to try and move it out of his way."

"Did you tell Micah?" I ask.

"No," Love reveals, lowering her head.

"Why not?" I ask.

"You know Micah would beat dude up if he found out," Ryann says.

"Do I need to make a visit to that school, or do I need to stop by John's office?" Mama asks. "You know I don't play that mess about my kids."

"No, I'm gonna deal with him myself," I answer.

I know the best way to deal with him, and it doesn't involve putting my hands on him, getting Micah involved, or having my mama make a visit anywhere. I know he doesn't believe I belong in AP Physics, or probably any AP classes at all, but I'm going to show him and everybody else why they shouldn't count me out. My focus is about to be unreal, and nothing or no one is going to get in my way. I'm not certain about a lot of things, but this is one thing I'm certain of.

"Your phone just vibrated," Love says, passing me my handbag that was placed in the chair beside her.

As I open my bag to find my phone, the screen is still lit and I can't believe the name I see on the screen. I just know I'm not seeing this correctly.

Young Rue: Meet me tonight.

~4~

Church Flow

"For where two or three gather together as my followers, I am there among them."
Matthew 18:20 NLT

Love

"So, who would like to open us up this evening?" Mrs. Stewart, our church's youth and young adult director asks. It's Wednesday night, so that means it's also teen Bible study night.

"I'll do it," Micah volunteers. "Please, bow your heads in prayer."

"Most gracious God, thank You for bringing us together once more. Thank You for giving us the desire to be in Your presence and to learn more about You. I pray that we learn something tonight that we can carry with us throughout the rest of the week and that we have a great time as we praise Your name. Father, bless everyone who came,

those who desired to come but couldn't, and those who are on their way. In Jesus' name, amen."

Just as Micah finishes with the prayer, Christian walks into the room with his brother Nehemiah. I just can't get over how handsome these brothers are. Christian has walked with me to class every day this week. However, he still hasn't asked for my number, so I'm a little bit confused. Does he really like me?

After he and Nehemiah grab the empty seats next to me and Truth, he says, "Good evening, Love Hudson."

"Good evening, Christian Carter."

"This is my brother, Nehemiah," he says. "Nehemiah, this is the one I've been telling you about." I can't believe he's been talking about me to his brother. I wonder what he has been saying.

"I hope he hasn't told you anything too terrible," I reply. "I'm Love, and it's nice to meet you. This is my twin, Truth."

"It's a pleasure meeting you both," Nehemiah says. His voice is slightly deeper than Christian's voice.

"It's a pleasure meeting you too, Nehemiah," Truth says, completely ignoring Christian. By the look in her eyes, I can tell she's plotting on how to woo Nehemiah.

"Well, I guess Love must've told you how much she dislikes me or something." Christian laughs, noticing how Truth didn't say it was a pleasure meeting him like it was meeting his brother.

"My bad! It was nice meeting you too, Christian," Truth says, shaking Christian's hand. "I've heard good stuff about you."

"Good stuff, huh?" Christian responds, amused. "Like what?"

"Oh, wouldn't you like to know?" Truth teases.

"Alright, y'all. Tonight's Bible study will be led by Brother Micah Hudson and Sister Joy Perez," Mrs. Stewart begins, causing all of our chatter to cease.

Joining Micah at the front of the room, Joy greets us by saying, "Good evening my brothers and sisters! Micah and I are thrilled to be leading tonight's Bible study. We're going to be talking about what it means to be unequally yoked." This sounds like this is going to be good. Us teens need to hear more about the dangers of being involved with unbelievers.

Following up, Micah says, "Our scripture reading for tonight comes from 2 Corinthians 6:14-15, and it reads 'Don't team up with those who are unbelievers. How can righteousness be a partner with wickedness? How can light live with darkness? What harmony can there be between Christ and the devil? How can a believer be a partner with an unbeliever?'"

Just as Micah finishes reading the scripture, Joel and Mercy creep into the room.

"Can anyone define a believer and an unbeliever?" Joy asks.

"A believer is someone who is living for God," Nehemiah answers.

"And an unbeliever is someone who isn't living for God," Christian adds.

"Great job, guys!" Joy says. "Does anyone know what it means to be unequally yoked?" Having read up on being unequally yoked plenty of times, I raise my hand.

"Yes, Love?" Micah acknowledges my raised hand.

"It refers to when a believer is joined together with an unbeliever," I answer.

"Good, sis," Micah compliments. "And why is being unequally yoked a bad thing for believer to do?"

"Because it's easier for an unbeliever to pull a believer down than it is for a believer to pull an unbeliever up," Christian replies.

"That's right, man." Micah nods. I can tell my brother is enjoying what Christian has to say.

"And that's why being unequally yoked is a terribly dangerous thing to do," Joy adds. "An unbeliever can easily cause us to stray away from God's plan for our lives."

"And most times we don't realize how bad it is to be unequally yoked with someone because we usually get into these situations with good intentions," Micah says. "We try to date someone to Christ, but in reality, only God can change an unbeliever's heart. We don't have the power by ourselves to change someone."

"But what if you're already deeply in love with someone before you realize that you might be unequally yoked?" Mercy asks. I wonder if she's referring to her and Joel. I'm not sure God is being completely glorified in their relationship, but that's none of my business.

"Good question, sis," Micah says. "Would you like to answer, Joy?"

"Sure," Joy agrees. "Mercy, no relationship with any boy, or girl for the guys in here, is worth your relationship with God. If the relationship isn't bringing you closer to Christ, cut him or her off. Period."

"I couldn't agree more with what Joy just said." Micah smiles.

"Thanks, Micah." Joy blushes. "A lot of you already know that Micah and I have been courting each other for a while now."

Raising her hand, Olivia says, "I know this might be a dumb question, but are courting and dating the same thing?" I invited Olivia to our church after our first cheer practice. She seems like such an innocent, young girl, and she reminds me of myself.

With Joy glancing at him, Micah responds, "No, courting and dating are two different things. Courting is the godly way of doing things. Courting seeks to glorify God, and the ultimate goal of a courtship is marriage."

"Can I also say something?" Christian politely interrupts.

"Yeah, go ahead man," Micah answers.

"Thanks," Christian says. "Dating seeks to please the flesh, and there are usually no boundaries when it comes to dating. You can date whoever you want whenever you want. You can sleep with whoever you want and however many people you want. Dating is an unbeliever's way of doing things. Dating isn't interested in glorifying God." Whoa, that was deep.

"Dang, man! You took the words right out of my mouth," Micah says.

"I'm impressed." Mrs. Stewart claps before being joined by everyone else.

When the applause dies, Joy starts up again, "As I was saying, a lot of you know that Micah and I have been courting for a while now. This was my first time actually being involved in a courtship, and it's been very rewarding so far. Not only do we go out together, but we also pray together, read our Bible together, and do other things to strengthen our walk with God."

"Since you guys are courting, do y'all feel like y'all are meant to be?" Olivia asks.

"Umm..." Joy blushes, struggling to find the right words to say.

Equally blushing, Micah answers, “The love I have for Joy is so real that I hope we’re meant to be. Luckily, our courtship allows our vision to not be clouded by feelings of lusting after only the physical aspects of the other. I’m in love with Joy’s mind, spirit, and devotion to God.”

The room erupts in “oohs” and “aahs.” Their relationship is literally so close to perfect that God has got to be doing some divine miracle work between them.

“Let’s continue, y’all.” Joy laughs. “Now we’re going to talk about boundaries in relationships/courtships that we recommend being put in place in order to help both partners maintain purity of mind and body.”

“First off, the Bible says that sex is to be reserved for married couples. Therefore, sex is off limits in a courtship,” Micah says.

“Not speaking of myself, but what if you aren’t a virgin anymore?” Mercy asks.

“If someone isn’t a virgin anymore, the first thing that he or she needs to do is turn to God and repent,” Joy answers.

“To repent means to completely turn away from something. Refraining from sexual sin after you’ve already committed it once might be hard, but you can do it. You just have to guard your heart and make sure you stay out of situations where you will be tempted to sin again,” Micah adds.

"I also want you to remember that you no longer being a virgin doesn't mean that God doesn't love you. We all make mistakes, but a mistake can be a lesson if you learn from it. However, it is my hope that y'all don't make the mistake of not waiting until marriage like I did," Joy reveals.

I didn't know Joy wasn't a virgin. Judging by the shocked faces staring her down, a lot of other people didn't know either, including Mercy.

"Is it ok for us to talk about this?" Joy asks Mrs. Stewart.

"Yes, go ahead," Mrs. Stewart urges. "We need to hear about this more in the church."

"First off, Micah and I have never had sex together. I lost my virginity my freshman year to this senior guy. Honestly, I was mostly attracted to him because he was a jock. All of the other girls wanted him, but I felt like I was the lucky one by actually having him. So stupid!"

"My faith in God wasn't as strong back then, and no one ever really told me that we should strive to wait until marriage. I always heard that sex was ok if you were in love, and I really thought I was in love. One night after his game, he was taking me home. Suddenly, he pulled over near this abandoned building and proceeded to tell me how much he loved me. I really believed him," Joy says with tears in her eyes.

Micah comforts her by grabbing onto her hand, and after a long pause Joy continues, "He started to kiss me and undress me right there in the front seat of his truck. It didn't take long because I wasn't wearing much. Back then, I thought I had to dress skimpy just to get and keep his attention on me and only me. Sadly, I was wrong. He had sex with me that night and told everyone about it the next day. I wasn't even embarrassed because I felt like it was such an achievement at the time. I felt like a woman. Then, I heard about him cheating on me with other girls, but I still stayed because I was blinded by good sex."

"We continued to have sex again and again until one night I told him I didn't want to keep doing it. He didn't want to hear it, so he raped me in the girls' bathroom after one of the basketball games. I felt so disgusting, powerless, and unworthy afterward. To make matters worse, he broke up with me the next morning."

I feel myself about to break down in tears. Hearing Joy's testimony for the first time has clearly touched everyone in this room. I never would have suspected that such a sweet, Christian girl like her had to go through something so terrible after losing her virginity to a trifling guy who would eventually rape her.

After Micah embraces her and wipes away her tears, Joy says, "I don't want y'all to feel sad for me. That wasn't my purpose for telling my story. I want y'all to learn from me. Sex won't keep someone around, and you're never too far gone for God to save you. With the help of Him, I've forgiven my rapist and moved past the pain of my past mistakes. You can do the same."

Amen.

After Bible study ends, everyone at church congregates inside the fellowship hall for refreshments and things. We have a variety of breads and cheeses, a large assortment of fruit, and grape juice and water.

"Tonight got a little deep," Truth says, strolling over to where I am standing along with Mercy.

"Yeah, it did," I reply. "The conversation needed to be had though."

"I agree," Christian says, popping out of nowhere with Nehemiah right behind him.

"I guess so," Mercy says, nonchalantly.

"Why did you have to say it like that?" Truth asks. Mercy's sister's testimony was so powerful, and for her to be acting so dismissive about it is a little rude.

"Say it like what?"

"Like you don't care," Truth responds.

"I do care," Mercy says. "I just don't think there's anything completely wrong with not waiting until marriage as long as you aren't giving it up too fast and to everybody."

"Whatever. You obviously missed the whole point." Truth dismisses the conversation and walks over to the food table.

“Whatever to you too!” Mercy yells behind her.

I should’ve said something to Mercy, but I know she’s just as headstrong as Truth is. I don’t know if what I have to say on the topic of sex before marriage is enough to change her views. I’ll make a mental note to pray for her though.

“I think I like her,” Nehemiah blurts out.

“You like who? Truth?” Mercy laughs.

“Yes. I like Truth,” Nehemiah says. This is shocking not only because Nehemiah seems so quiet and reserved, but also because Truth seems like the total opposite of someone you’d expect him to be attracted to.

“Do you want me to tell her?” I laugh too.

“No thanks, Love,” he responds. “I’ll do it when I feel like the time is right.”

“I see you, bro!” Christian fist bumps Nehemiah.

“Chill, man,” Nehemiah responds.

“That’s cool though,” I say. “My sister might be a little rough around the edges, but she has a good heart.”

“I bet she does,” Nehemiah says before moving over to where Truth is.

After a couple of minutes, Christian asks me, “Can I ask you something in private, Love?”

“Sure,” I answer. “Mercy, do you mind?”

“Oh no! I’m about to head out with Joel anyways,” she responds, walking over to where Micah, Joel, Nehemiah, and some of the other athletes are now conversing.

When she's out of earshot, I ask, "What's going on, Christian?"

Nervously sweating he says, "I was just wondering if you would like to go out this weekend."

"Like go out together?" I reply.

"Ha! What else, Love?" he says. "Of course go out together."

"Umm, I don't know, Christian. My parents don't actually let us date yet."

"Have you ever asked them could you go out with anyone?"

"They've always told us that we couldn't date until we were sixteen," I admit.

"Well, that's probably because they haven't met me, and you're almost sixteen anyways." Christian smiles. "I'm about to go ask your dad myself."

"No you're not!" I respond, but I'm too late. He's already sprinting toward my daddy who happens to be on the opposite side of the room.

My daddy doesn't even know him, so he's definitely going to say no. There's no way he's letting me go out with him, and there's nothing Christian can do to change that. He might have the ability to woo me, but he isn't going to have the same luck with Daddy.

When I'm in earshot of Daddy and Christian, I hear Christian saying, "Hi Pastor Hudson. I'm Christian Carter." He firmly shakes Daddy's hand. "I wanted to let you know that I thoroughly enjoyed your sermon on Sunday."

"Thanks, young man! It's a pleasure meeting you," Daddy says. "Are you new to the area? I don't think I've met you and your family before."

"I'm not new here, but last week was my first time attending church here," Christian responds. "I brought my twin brother with me tonight."

"Well, I'm glad to have you here, Christian, and if you don't have a church home, please consider joining our fellowship."

"Thanks a lot, Pastor Hudson," Christian says. "You'll definitely be seeing a lot of my brother and me."

"You said twin brother, right?" Daddy asks.

"Yes sir," Christian politely answers.

"I have twin daughters myself," Daddy says to Christian, unaware that we're already quite acquainted. "Have you met Love and Truth?"

"Umm..." Christian begins.

"Oh, wait! There's one of them over there." Daddy notices me spying from a short distance. "Come here, Love!"

Lord, what am I getting myself into?

Reluctantly walking over, I say, "Hi, Daddy."

"Hey, baby. This young man here is Christian Carter, and he's new to our service," Daddy says.

"Daddy, I know him already," I nervously admit. "We go to school together."

"Oh! Why didn't you tell me, young brother?" Daddy nudges Christian.

"I was just about to tell you," Christian says. "She's actually one of the reasons why I came over here to introduce myself."

"And why is that?" Daddy asks with a raised brow.

"Please, don't do this," I silently mouth to Christian.

"I was wondering if it would be ok for your daughters, my brother, and I to hang out together this weekend," Christian says. "He doesn't have any friends here, and your daughters seem to be two nice young ladies."

Without hesitation, my dad says, "That sounds like a great idea to me!" What? I'm totally confused right now. I thought we couldn't date until we were sixteen!

"Thanks!" Christian exclaims. "But only if it's ok with Love and Truth."

"Love, what do you say?" Daddy looks down at me.

After clearing my throat, I say, "Sure, that's fine with me."

"Thanks, Love!" Christian shakes my hand. "Should we exchange numbers?"

"Yes, make sure you do that," Daddy answers for me.

Having the ok from my dad, Christian asks, "What's your number, Love? I'll put it in my cell and text you mine."

"Ok," I say before giving him my number.

"You can pick the girls up from our house this weekend, or I can drop them off," Daddy says.

"We can pick them up," Christian says. "My brother and I both drive."

"It was really nice meeting you, Christian." Daddy embraces Christian in a man-hug and walks off to join my mom and some of our other church members.

"I can't wait, Love." Christian smiles.

"Me either." I smile back before waving goodbye.

~5~

Knowing Better

"Keep me from lying to myself; give me the privilege of knowing your instructions."
Psalms 119:29 NLT

Mercy

After turning on the latest Rihanna song, I buckle up my seatbelt and wait for Joel to return to the car. He went back inside the fellowship hall to get his backpack. I wish he would hurry up because I'm so ready to go.

I wasn't feeling church tonight. I'm upset that this was my first time hearing about my sister losing her virginity and being raped. Given that I'm her sister and supposedly her best friend, I would have expected to be one of the first people she revealed all of this to, but I guess I was wrong.

Suddenly, Joel's phone begins to vibrate from inside his driver's side door. When I reach over to grab it, I notice an unsaved number calling. I wonder who this is, but he's my man so I'm sure he doesn't care if I answer.

"Hello?" I say into the phone.

No one says anything, but I hear snickers coming from the other end. As a matter of fact, they sound like the snickers of females.

"Who is this?" I ask, getting an attitude. Quickly, the voice or voices on the other end of the phone hang up.

Literally a second later, Joel reenters his car saying, "Mercy, what are you doing with my phone?"

Lord, was that bass I heard in his voice?

"Oh, so it's a problem for me to answer your phone?"

"You don't ever see me picking up yours," Joel shouts, snatching his phone away from me.

"Really, Joel?" I can't believe he's acting this way. "Just take me home."

"Home? I thought we were going over to my crib."

"The keyword is 'were.' Take me home now!" I respond.

Unexpectedly, Joel attempts to slide his hand underneath my skirt, but I stop him right in his tracks. It's obvious that he wasn't paying attention in church tonight, like Truth accused me of not doing.

"Joel, what do you think you're doing? I said take me home!"

"You know what, Mercy? Nevermind! Just nevermind."

"Nevermind what?"

"I'm so sick of this," Joel unsuccessfully attempts to mutter underneath his breath.

"I heard you," I respond, but he doesn't say anything.

The rest of the ride to my house is silent. Joel doesn't say anything to me, and I don't say anything to him either. Maybe I was wrong for answering his phone, and maybe I was wrong for stopping him from reaching under my skirt. After all, I am his girlfriend. Aren't I supposed to let him do things like that?

Abruptly, Joel stops his car in front of my house. It was as if he was going to pass by it or something before realizing what he was doing.

"Umm..." I say, waiting for Joel to come over to the passenger's side to open the door for me.

"What?" Joel smacks his lips, obviously still upset with me.

"Whatever, Joel." I get out and slam the door.

As I march up my driveway, Joel speeds off. He has never been this way with me. He usually helps me out of his car and walks me to my door, but tonight he didn't do any of that just because he's mad at me. I want to feel bad for upsetting him, but he'll be alright. No matter how mad he gets, I know he can't stay mad at me for long.

Unlocking the door to the house, I feel a little bit a relief. I can't wait to go up to my room and prepare for bed. It's going to be an early night for me.

As soon as I walk through the door, my mother greets me, "Hi, Mercy. How was church?"

"It was fine," I respond. "Why weren't you there with Daddy?"

"I was just tired, baby."

"That's not a good excuse."

Ignoring my comment, Mom asks, "Where's Joy? Didn't you ride together?"

"No, actually we didn't. I rode with Joel."

"Oh."

"Oh what?" I ask.

"Your father and I have something that we need to talk to you about?" Mom says.

"Please tell me it's not about Joel." I roll my eyes. I don't have time for this tonight. I really just want to get to bed. Plus, I need to flexi-rod my hair tonight, and I know that's going to take up most of my time.

"No, honey," she replies.

"Well, what is it about?"

"It's about you."

"What about me?"

"Please wait until your father gets home," she says, looking out the window. It looks like something is bothering her.

"Mom, are you ok?" I probe.

"Yes, I'm fine," she says.

Just as I'm about to ask my mom another question, I hear a car pull up. I don't know if it's my father or Joy, but I know it's one of them.

A minute or so later, my father and Joy walk through the door with huge smiles on their faces. However, these smiles only last momentarily as they notice my mom's face.

"Hey, Mom. What's wrong?" Joy asks.

Seeming to already know what's going on, my father says, "Joy, go to your room. We need to have a talk with Mercy."

"Yes sir," Joy says and proceeds to go upstairs to her room.

"Daddy, what's wrong?" I ask.

"We heard about you being late to school the other day," my daddy says in that stern tone of his.

Thinking of a quick lie, I say, "I was having a hard time finding the classroom." I already know they're talking about me being late to homeroom the other day. Miss Mason must have told my mom.

"Mercy, don't lie to us," Mom says.

"I'm not lying!" I rise indignantly.

"Miss Mason told me that you said you were having car trouble, and we know that's not true," Mom responds.

I roll my eyes. "I thought you said that this wasn't about me and Joel?"

"I said it wasn't about Joel. It's about you," Mom replies. "You need to start making better decisions, Mercy. That boy is no good for you."

"And how would you know?" I raise my voice.

"Mercy, watch your tone," Daddy says. "We just want what's best for you."

"How do you know what's best for me?"

"Mercy, we've been there and done that, so we know what we're talking about," Mom says.

"And I was a boy that age once. He wants more than what you might be prepared to give," Daddy says.

"Gosh, I'm not stupid!" I shout.

"We know you're not stupid," Mom says. "We raised you right, and we don't want you to forget what we've taught you. I've seen it happen too often to young girls at that school."

"So, what do you expect me to do, Mom? Break up with Joel? That's not happening for you or for anyone."

"Mercy, listen to me—"

"I'm done listening for the night," I say, interrupting my mom.

With that being said, I grab my keys and storm out of the house. I don't know where I'm going, but I'm going somewhere far away from here.

After driving for a while, I finally glance at my phone. It's hard to believe only an hour or so has passed by, and I have eleven missed calls. Eight of them are from my mother, two of them are from my daddy, and one of them is from Joy. To be honest, I still don't want to talk to either of them.

As I pull into the parking lot of Sarah's Sub Shack, I can't help but wish I had someone to comfort me. I decide I might as well call my boyfriend.

After what seems like endless ringing, I decide to hang up the phone and try again. Still no answer. I guess he's still mad. That's just perfect. I guess I'll try one of my girls.

"Hello?" Truth answers.

"Girl, what's up?" I ask. Hopefully she can take my mind off of this mess at home with the latest tea or something. I know we had a little argument earlier, but maybe she has forgotten all about that.

"Can you come pick me up ASAP?"

"Funny!" I fake laugh. "Don't you like have curfew or something?"

"Yeah, but I'm sneaking out."

"To go where?"

"To meet Young Rue, and you're coming with me."

"You said what?" I want to clarify. The last thing I heard was that she hadn't even heard from him, but now, all a sudden, she's sneaking out to meet up with him. This girl is wild, but I guess that's why we're best friends.

"You heard me," she says. "We, as in you and me, are hanging out with Rue and his boys tonight."

Thinking about my situation at home and my situation with Joel, I decide that a little fun tonight doesn't sound like a bad idea.

"Count me in! I'm on my way." I hang up the phone and speed out of the parking lot.

When I make it to the twins' street, I send Truth a text message.

Mercy: I'm at the stop sign down the street.

Truth: Cool, I'm omw now.

Truth texted me her escape plan while I was on my way over. They live in a massive, three-story home in Buckhead, so it shouldn't be too hard for her to sneak out. Truth and Love both have rooms on the third floor, their parents have a room on the second floor, and Micah has a room on the first floor. Getting by her parents shouldn't be the hard part, but Micah might pose a problem. Luckily, he's probably sleeping or too busy on the phone talking to Joy to hear Truth sneak out. I know for sure that Love is already sleeping though. She goes to bed so early.

Like three minutes later, I notice a thin, dark figure marching toward my car. I was so lost in my thoughts that I didn't realize it was Truth.

"Unlock the door, girl!" Truth bangs on the window.

"Dang! Don't rush me."

"Shut up," she replies, taking a seat in my car.

"So what's the next move?" I ask, trying to mask my excitement.

"Rue offered to pick us up from my crib, but I told him we could meet him at his crib."

"Did he give you an address?" I'm quite interested to see where he lives.

"Yeah, it's 52 Cherokee Rose Cove," Truth answers. "Want me to type it into the GPS?"

"Of course, honey!"

After typing it into the GPS on her phone, Truth says, "Oh, it's not even that far. It's only six minutes away."

"So, you mean to tell me your family is so rich that you live in the same neighborhood as rappers?" I joke.

"Shut up." Truth brushes off my comment. "What's wrong with you though?"

"What makes you think something is wrong with me?" I ask, knowing my demeanor is a little different tonight.

"First of all, you were tripping earlier tonight. Second of all, you're out a little late for a school night. Third of all, if everything was fine, you'd probably be somewhere talking to Joel. Fourth of all—"

"Ok!" I interrupt. "You've made your point."

After a long pause, she asks, "So are you going to tell me what's wrong with you or not?"

"Everything," I answer, not ready to tell her everything that has happened tonight.

"Quit playing with me, Mercy. Tell me what's going on."

"Ugh ok!" I give in. "Joel is mad at me because I wouldn't let him feel me up, and my parents tried to force me to break up with him. Great night, huh?"

"Dang." Truth stares at me shocked. "You told them what he did?"

"Heck no. That would give them even more reason to hate him."

"But are you ok though?" Truth asks, looking concerned.

"Not yet, but I will be soon," I assure her. "Let's talk about something else though."

She hits me in the arm. "Girl, let me tell you what's going down this weekend!"

"Ouch!" I hit her back. "What's going on?"

"Apparently, I have a date with Nehemiah this weekend."

"Hold on! What? I knew he said he liked you, but I thought he was going to wait to ask you out."

"What are you talking about?" Truth asks, making me realize I might have said too much considering that Nehemiah doesn't want his crush on Truth to be known yet. "Christian asked my daddy if he and Nehemiah could take Love and me out this weekend."

"Wait, he actually asked your dad?"

"Yep, that's what Love said," Truth says. "I'm kinda curious to see how this goes. He gave me his number after church."

"Seriously?"

"Yeah."

"Are you going to use it?"

"It depends on how tonight goes with Rue."

"Ok," I say, making a right turn into the open gateway that leads to the driveway of this large mansion. "I think this is it, Truth."

"Dang! This crib is nice," Truth says, admiring Rue's place.

His place even looks like it belongs to a rapper. Behind a large, circular driveway sits this gigantic house that's about three stories high with a five-car garage attached. My favorite part about the place is the large balcony overlooking the city.

"Rue must be loaded if he can afford this place," I say. "If you don't take him, I will."

"Girl bye!" she exclaims as I park my car near the cars already parked out front. "You ready?"

"I think so. How do I look?"

"Put on some more lipstick, and you'll be alright."

"Will do," I say, reaching into my handbag for my new matte red lipstick.

"What do I look like?" Truth asks.

"Flawless, honey!" I smile. "That hair of yours is laid to the gods."

"You know how I do." She laughs, doing a slight flip of the hair. "Now let's go."

Exiting the car, I feel thrilled. I don't know what's about to go down tonight, but I am ready for it all. I need this after the night I've had.

As soon as we make it to the large door at the entrance of the house, Truth hesitates for a minute and asks, "Should I ring the doorbell?"

"I don't know, Truth! Call him or something."

While Truth calls Rue, I check my phone. I don't have any new calls, texts, or anything. I'm not worried about hearing from my family right now, but I am wondering why Joel hasn't responded to my call. He can't possibly still be mad. Since he wants to act this way though, I'm about to do some stuff tonight that I may or may not regret later.

"Hey, we're here," Truth says into the phone.

"What's he saying?" I whisper, excitedly grabbing her arm.

"Ok," she says into the phone.

"So?" I ask.

"Stop acting like a groupie," Truth says. "He said come on in. They're in the basement."

"You go first." I push her.

As soon as Truth opens the door, the aroma of food, alcohol, and weed hits us. I haven't been in the presence of weed many times, but I know the smell when I come into contact with it. It smells like a skunk.

"Let's just follow the smell," Truth says.

We walk through the doorway and immediately see this big, beautiful staircase covered in gold. It's one of those circular stairways that I've always thought were classy. Rue must have a good eye.

"I think these stairs lead to the basement," Truth says, interrupting my admiration of the house.

"Most likely," I say, following Truth to the stairs but still scoping out my surroundings.

"The smell is definitely getting louder this way," she says.

Strutting down the steps one by one like the queen I am, I try to hide the fact that I'm so excited to be around Young Rue and his crew. I'm glad I left the house still looking good.

"What's up, shawty?" Some guy hugs Truth as we make it to the basement. I can't really see in this dark room, but I assume it's Young Rue.

"Hey, how are you?" Truth greets the guy back. "This is my best friend Mercy."

"What's up, Mercy?" The guy shakes my hand. "I'm Rue."

"It's nice to meet you, Rue," I reply, still trying to mask my excitement. I can't believe it's actually Young Rue.

"Likewise." Rue nods his head. "Let me introduce y'all to my boys."

There are like three other guys in the room, and they all look to be around the same age as Rue. They all look good on the eyes, too, might I add.

"Y'all, meet Truth and Mercy," Rue introduces us. "They came to kick it with us tonight."

"Hey, I'm Dame," says this medium-sized, brown-skinned, tatted guy in a Hawks jersey.

"I'm Mack," the chubby, handsome one wearing a white tee and basketball shorts says.

"What's up? I'm Jesse," says the tall, light-skinned, dread head that I've had my eyes on since I walked in. He's dressed in a black button-down shirt with some dark jeans, which I consider to be very dapper.

"What's up?" Truth and I reply in unison.

"Y'all are beautiful." Mack smiles, showcasing every single tooth in his mouth. "You know they call me Mack because I'm good with the ladies."

"Chill, man. This one is mine." Rue grabs Truth by the waist, causing her to blush like a middle schooler.

"Aw, I see you my boy!" Mack responds.

"Ladies, feel free to make yourself comfortable," Rue says. "I'm finna head upstairs to get some more drinks." I've never drank before, and I know Truth hasn't either. Fortunately, I'm looking for a good time, so I don't mind trying my first drink tonight.

"Mercy, you have a unique name," Jesse compliments me. "You should come join me over here."

Without hesitation, I take a seat next to him on the black, leather sofa. I don't get too close to him because I don't want him to think I'm thirsty for his attention.

"You must be waiting on Rue to get back?" Jesse says to Truth. "You know you can join us too."

"My bad," Truth says, heading to claim a seat next to me.

"I was gonna ask if y'all wanted to hit the weed, but it seems like you're already out of there, Truth," Dame says, taking a jab at Truth.

"I don't smoke," Truth replies.

"What about you, Mercy?" Jesse asks.

"Honestly, weed has never really been appealing to me," I respond, failing to admit that I've never smoked a day in my life. They don't need to know that. I've heard too many stories of people coming across bad weed.

"Me either," Rue says, returning from upstairs with drinks and cups in tow.

"Really?" Truth asks.

"Yes really," Rue answers. "I don't smoke or drink."

"Is he lying?" I ask Jesse.

"He's telling the truth," Jesse says.

"I have no reason to lie." Rue throws his hands up in innocence. "Mack and Dame are the only ones who smoke and drink here."

"I'm shocked," I respond. "Why do you rap about drinking and smoking weed then?"

"To be honest, that's the type of music that sells. I'm just trying to keep my family out the hood."

"That's understandable," I say.

"Let's get this party started now y'all," Mack says with a large bottle already in his hand.

As Rue turns on his latest hit, the guys rise from their seats. There is a pool table, an air hockey table, one of those arcade basketball games, a collection of video games and various consoles in front of this massive flat screen television, and a large spread of food and drinks on the other side of the room.

"You want a sip, Truth?" Mack asks with his bottle lifted in the air.

"Nah, I'm good," Truth replies.

"I think we should've brought some Kool-Aid for the girls," Dame jokes, making the rest of the guys laugh.

"Who said I wasn't drinking?" I ask. I don't want to seem like a wimp.

"Let me pour you something then, baby." Jesse successfully pulls me over to the table with the liquor.

"Sounds good," I reply.

"Here's a shot of tequila." Jesse hands me a small glass filled with liquor.

"Thanks," I say, acting like it's not my first time drinking.

To be honest, the drink looks a little too much like pee and smells like musk. To avoid looking at it and smelling it any longer, I swallow it quickly. The taste feels like fire blazing my throat, and it doesn't taste good. However, I feel invigorated and want more.

"Dang, you drunk that fast," Dame says.

"I was just about to say the same thing." Jesse looks impressed. "Do you want another one?"

"Of course," I answer, nonchalantly. Out of the corner of my eye, I notice Truth glaring at me.

"Here you go." Jesse places my refilled shot glass into my hand.

Just as quickly as I swallowed the first shot, I swallow the second shot. Two shots in two minutes isn't so bad, right?

"I guess I'm not the only alcoholic in the room," Mack says, still clinging to his large bottle of alcohol.

"Whatever," I reply.

"Are you going for three?" Jesse asks with a smug look on his face. Gosh, he looks so good to me.

Before I can answer, Truth demands, "Come here, Mercy."

Feeling a little woozy already, I nearly stumble in my heels making it over to where Truth and Rue are standing.

When I make it over there, I ask, “What’s up, chica?”

Pulling me away from Rue, she asks, “What the heck is wrong with you?”

Even though she whispered it, I can feel the anger emanating from her voice. I’m sure she would’ve yelled at me if we weren’t in a room filled with guys.

“What do you mean?” I ask.

“You’re drinking, and you know you’re the one driving,” Truth says. “I ought to slap you upside your head.”

“Relax, Truth,” I slowly enunciate as I slap her shoulder.

“Mercy, do not play with me!” Truth says.

Sensing the tension, Rue interrupts Truth’s madness saying, “Truth and I are about to go out on the balcony to talk for a minute. Feel free to continue what y’all were doing.”

“I’ll be back. Don’t do nothing stupid,” Truth says, glaring at me the whole time as Rue leads her from the basement.

Walking back over to the alcohol table where Jesse and Mack are standing, I start to feel a little aggravated. Truth is upset, disappointed, or something, but she knows I came here to have fun. She needs to loosen up a bit.

“Let’s play a game!” Mack suggests, obviously drunk already.

"I'm down," Dame says. "First say what's up to Snapchat."

As he pans the room with his phone recording a video, I wonder how many followers he has on Snapchat. He begins with Mack who flashes his bottle. Then, he gets Jesse who flashes a sexy smile while chucking up the deuces.

When Dame puts his camera on me, he says "Say what's up to the homie Mercy."

I just smile, wave, and say, "Add me at MamiMercy."

When the video is done recording, Dame says, "Let's get on this game."

"What game are we playing, man?" Jesse asks.

"Let's play Never Have I Ever," Mack says.

"How do you play?" I ask.

"Everybody has to say something they've never done before," Mack begins to explain.

"Then if you've done it before, you have to take a sip of whatever's in your glass," Dame adds.

"Or bottle." Mack flashes his bottle yet again.

"I thought you didn't drink though?" I say to Jesse.

"I don't," he says. "I'll just fill my cup with some orange juice instead."

"Oh ok," I reply, eager to begin playing this game. "Fill my glass again please."

"I'll go first," Dame offers as Jesse pours me another shot of tequila. "Never have I ever worn a skirt." The boys laugh because I'm the only female in the room, and I'm currently wearing a skirt.

Following the rules of the game, I take my third shot of tequila.

"I'm next," Mack says. "Never have I ever worn a bra."

"Are you sure man?" Dame says, and we all laugh.

"Man, forget you!" Mack responds. "The females love my man boobs."

"That's what you think." Dame fans him off. "Take your shot, Mercy!"

I'm feeling a little tipsy right now, so I know the alcohol is kicking in in my system. I don't know how many more shots I can take, but I take this one anyways.

Noticing the discomfort written on my face, Jesse says, "How about we shoot some pool? I'm not really feeling this game right now."

"Y'all can play," Dame responds. "I'm just gonna chill on the couch and watch."

"I think I'll just watch, too," I say. I don't know how to shoot pool.

"I guess it's just me and Mack then." Jesse feigns disappointment. "Can you at least cheer me on, Mercy?"

"Of course, boo." I flirtatiously bat my eyelashes.

After a few minutes of watching Jesse and Mack play, I still have no idea what's going on. I can't seem to maintain my focus.

"Hey, Mercy," Mack says. "I dare you to do something."

"Something like what?"

"If Jesse makes this shot, I dare you to take your shirt off," he responds. I'm caught off guard with this dare, and I don't know if it's the alcohol in me, the pain I've felt tonight, or what, but I'm feeling a little daring tonight.

"Sure. I don't think he'll make it, though," I playfully tease.

Jesse doesn't say anything, but he does give me this sly smile before making what appears to be an easy shot.

"Uh-oh!" Mack says. "You know what that means."

"Strip," Dame says.

Jesse appears to be waiting to see if I'm going to do what I agreed to, so I crawl onto the pool table. Since I'm taking my top off, I might as well give them a little show, right?

Once I'm on top of the pool table, I stand all the way up and begin playing with my hair and swaying my hips to the smooth beat of the music coming through the speakers of the stereo system. When I notice that Jesse is completely focused on what I'm doing, I yank my shirt over my head and throw it his way. He catches it, too.

When I climb off of the pool table, I nearly stumble. Luckily, Jesse is there to catch me.

"You have a nice body, Mercy," he whispers into my ear, gently gripping my waist. Cheerleading helps me stay in shape, but working out a little bit on my own doesn't hurt either. I know my small frame and 4-pack abs are looking mighty fine right now.

"Thanks," I whisper back in his ear.

"Let's finish this game," Jesse says to Mack before letting me go.

While the guys resume their pool match, I decide to just chill out to the music playing. Rue is a pretty decent rapper. His smooth beats and occasional singing distract you from the dirty lyrics that are coming from his mouth.

"Mercy, somebody's Facetiming you," Dame says. I forgot I left my phone over there on the couch.

"Who is it?" I ask.

"Somebody named Joel," Dame says. "Want me to answer it?" I assume he's joking, but it would be a good way to get back at Joel for the way that he acted tonight.

"Yeah, answer it!" I smile, ready to get a reaction out of my so-called boyfriend.

Once the Facetime call is connected, Dame greets Joel saying, "What's up?"

"Who the heck are you?" I hear Joel yell into the phone.

"It's Dame, and I'm with Young Rue, DJ Mack, Jesse, and your girl Mercy."

After yelling a few obscene words, Joel says, “Put Mercy on the phone now!”

“Say hi, Mercy.” Dame turns the camera onto me as I continue to dance close to Jesse.

Gosh! I forgot that I was still topless. Joel is going to freak out, but I don’t care right now.

“Hi, Joel,” I say as I proceed to kiss Jesse, which catches us both by surprise.

“Are you sure about this, Mercy?” Jesse stops me.

“Yeah, I’m s-s-sure,” I respond, noticing that the alcohol is affecting me a bit more now.

“Fine,” Jesse responds before softly pushing me against the wall parallel to the pool table.

“Your friend just hung up,” Dame informs me, but I continue to kiss Jesse as if I couldn’t care less.

I ignore him because I honestly don’t care right now. I’ve been so hurt today by both Joel and my family, and Jesse is the only thing distracting me from all of the hurt in my heart. I know better than to be doing this, but this feels so good. I deserve to feel good, right?

~6~

Rich and Famous

"The rich and the poor have this in common: The lord made them both."

Proverbs 22:2 NLT

Truth

"What are you thinking about, Truth?" Rue asks, breaking me out of the daze I was in.

We have been standing on his balcony talking for the past hour, and I'm loving every moment of it. It reminds me of our first night together in Florida. It's nice and cool out, and I've told him my whole life story up until this point. There's something different about him, but I still don't know much about him.

"To be real, I'm thinking about you," I say as I continue to stare at the bright city lights.

"What about me?"

"Tell me about you," I say. "I want to know more."

"What do you wanna know?"

"I don't know. Just tell me something."

"Honestly, I have a hard time opening up to people."

"And why is that?" I ask.

"Every time I let someone get too close, they let me down," Rue says. "And it all started with my sperm donor."

"What happened?" I ask.

"Truth, if you keep it real with me, I'll keep it real with you. Ok?"

"Ok," I say, confused as to how this answers my question.

"You should probably get going," he says, confusing me even further. I thought we were having a good time and that the night was just beginning. I don't know if he's trying to avoid my question or what. Either way, I don't like it.

"Why do you say that?" I can't help but ask.

"Because you have school in the morning."

How did he even know I was still in school? I purposely left out that small detail.

"Am I right or wrong?" He laughs.

Lowering my head in embarrassment, I respond, "You're right."

"So how old are you, Truth?" He turns his head toward me.

"I'm almost 16," I answer truthfully. That sounds better than saying I'm 15.

"Aw cool," he responds.

I hope this doesn't change things between us.

After he doesn't say anything for a couple of minutes, I ask, "Do you still want to keep talking or is that a problem with you?"

Smiling, he says, "It's not like I'm trying to sleep with you or something. You're cool, Truth."

"Good." I breathe a sigh of relief.

"Good that you're cool or good that I'm not trying to sleep with you?" Rue laughs again.

"Both."

"I can respect that." Rue nods. "Should we head back inside?"

"Yeah let's do that." I rub the goose bumps on my arm. "I was getting kinda cold, but I didn't want to say anything."

"Me too. I hope your friend didn't mind me snatching you away from her tonight."

"She knows how to handle her own."

Walking down the stairs to the basement, nothing could have prepared me for the shock I was about to receive.

"Mercy, what the heck are you doing?!" I scream. I don't know what has been going on while Rue and I were away, but we come back and see Mercy and Jesse sprawled out on the pool table. Both of them are shirtless, and it looks like they were minutes away from having sex right in front of everyone.

"Jesse, man what's going on?" Rue asks.

Both of them stare back. Mercy looks startled to see us standing here, but Jesse plays it cool.

"I think they need a room." Dame laughs, but I don't see anything funny about this pitiful situation.

Grabbing my drunk friend off the top of the pool table, I say, "Let's go. Now!"

"Wait a minute," Rue says, grabbing my arm.

"Wait for what?"

"Didn't Mercy drive?" Rue asks.

"Yeah, but I can get us back home," I respond, not believing the words I just said.

"I don't think so," Rue replies. "Let me drive y'all."

"That's not the best idea," I say, not wanting to be caught with him by Mercy's parents or my own family.

"Well, can I at least call an Uber for y'all?" he asks. "It's the least I can do."

After taking a moment to consider his offer, I say, "Sure you can do that. My address is 8 Moriah Cove."

"Ok, I'll request the Uber right now."

"What about Mercy's car though?" I ask.

"Y'all can come and get it when she's feeling better or I can have it towed to her house for her," Rue says.

If we come and get it, we'll have to find a ride here tomorrow. Mercy is the only one out of our clique who has a car, so we would have to either tell my brother or her sister to bring us here. I don't want them finding out about any of this though. However, if we have Mercy's car towed, we still might have to answer to some questions. We'll either have to lie, which I don't want to do, or we'll have to tell the truth about why Mercy's car had to be towed unless there's a discreet way to do all of this.

After considering my options for a little while longer, I say to Rue, "We'll just come and get it tomorrow."

"Ok. Just let me know when y'all are on the way, and I'll make sure I'm here," Rue says. I don't know how we'll get back here tomorrow, but we'll have to figure something out.

"Thank you." I sigh, still pissed.

"You're welcome," he says, embracing me in a hug.

I still can't believe I'm here with him right now, and I really can't believe it's possible that I could be the future girlfriend of one of the hottest rappers in Atlanta.

Slowly loosening our embrace, Rue says, "Y'all guys can leave now."

"What man?" Mack grabs another bottle. "I thought the party was just getting started!" He's so drunk right now.

"Nah," Rue replies. "It's time for y'all to go."

Jesse is the first one to move. He hangs his head and silently heads out of the basement. Shortly after, Mack and Dame stumble up the stairs after him. I'm assuming that Jesse is going to be the one driving them home since he's the only one that appears to be sober.

Glancing at his phone, Rue says, "The Uber will be here soon, so we might as well head upstairs too."

"Alright," I respond, feeling exhausted.

Mercy makes her way to the stairs, not saying anything. I'm trying to decide if I want to let her have it when we get in the car or if I want to just give her the silent treatment the whole way home.

Exiting Rue's mansion, the cool breeze hits me like a slap in the face. Immediately, I start shivering.

Right on time, Rue pulls me into his warm embrace and whispers into my ear, "Despite everything, I hope you enjoyed yourself tonight. I know I did."

I'm thankful it's dark outside and that Mercy is walking ahead of us because I know I'm blushing so hard right now, which I usually don't do. His words sent a chill down my spine that's even cooler than this breeze out here.

"Thanks," I respond. "I did have a good time chilling with you again."

"I hope we can do it again sometime." Rue smiles and places his jacket around my shoulders.

"When?" I ask, feeling hopeful.

"Soon," he replies. "I really can't say when because I'm gonna be busy these next few weeks with my music, performing, interviewing, and stuff, but I'll let you know."

Disappointed with Rue's response, I answer saying, "I understand."

"Do you?"

"I think so."

Turning me around so I can face him, Rue says, "I know you've never dealt with anyone in the industry before, and I just wanna keep it real with you. I'm busy a lot, so I probably won't be as available as you need me to be."

"I under—"

"No," Rue interrupts me. "Let me finish."

"Ok."

"I just want to make sure you understand because I don't want you to feel like I'm just another heartless dude out here. That's not who I am," he says. "I like who you are and the energy you bring, and I don't wanna leave you alone. Like I said, I might not be as available to you as you'd like, but I'm gonna do what I can when I can."

"I can respect that." I nod, noticing a car creeping up Rue's long driveway.

"Thank you."

"You're welcome," I reply.

I don't know what I'm getting myself into. I'll admit that I was attracted to Rue in the beginning only because he was a sexy rapper. Now I see there's something else that attracts me to him. I don't even know what it is, but maybe it's the mysteriousness surrounding him. I'm so used to being the one who breaks heart, but I'm scared that this time around I might be the one who ends up with the broken heart.

When the Uber pulls up in front of us, Mercy immediately gets in. She doesn't even tell Rue thank you or good night. I'll make sure not to bring her around him again anytime soon aside from coming to get her car tomorrow.

"I guess this is good night, Truth." Rue hugs me.

"Good night." I return his embrace, not wanting to let go yet.

We stay this way for a little while longer, but when he lets me go he kisses me on the forehead. I want to go for his lips. However, I'll settle for this.

Guiding me into the Uber, Rue says, "Good night, Mercy. See you later, Truth."

Before he closes the door, I ask, "Do you want your jacket back?"

"No," he says. "Keep it to remember me when I'm not around."

"I will," I respond as he gently closes the car door.

When we're safely off of Rue's property, Mercy says, "Truth, please let me expl—"

"Shut up!" I exclaim, my anger resurfacing. "I don't want to hear nothing you have to say right now. You embarrassed me tonight, and you embarrassed yourself."

"I'm sor—"

"I don't wanna hear it!" I cut her off again.

The rest of the short ride back to my house was completely quiet. Mercy was quiet. I was quiet. Even the Uber driver was quiet.

When the driver reaches the same stop sign that Mercy met me at earlier, I tell him, “Here is fine.”

“Sure?” he asks.

“Yeah, I’m sure,” I respond, unbuckling my seatbelt. “Thank you. Good night.”

Exiting the car, I realize Mercy is exiting too.

“I guess you’re not going home, huh?”

“I can’t go back there,” she says, staring at the ground. “I especially can’t go back without my car. Can I crash at your place?”

“Sure, whatever.”

Usually I would’ve been glad to have my girl over, but tonight I don’t even want to look at her anymore. I’m still having a hard time believing that she stooped so low tonight. Mercy is such a classy girl, but tonight she behaved like a straight-up groupie.

Sneaking out was a lot easier than I expected, so I’m sure sneaking back in will be even easier. Although I now have Mercy with me, my parents and siblings should be knocked out right now, so they won’t hear a thing.

***

It’s Thursday afternoon, and the entire school is buzzing. Apparently, last night Mercy was on Dame’s Snapchat story with Mack and Jesse. I knew how popular Rue was, but I didn’t know his friends were well known too. Because of it, Mercy has been the talk of the school all day, and it’s getting on my last nerve. I was the reason she even got to meet them in the first place.

Last night, we went straight to bed after we snuck in. I slept in my bed, but I suggested that Mercy sleep in the guestroom instead of my room. That was a petty move on my part, but I just didn't feel like being around her any longer. Now, I can't even stop hearing her name. Someone in every one of my classes has mentioned her name.

I decided to skip lunch today to sit outside alone on one of the benches for a little bit. I can't stop thinking about the time I spent with Rue last night, but I also had a pop quiz in my AP World History class this morning. I didn't study at all last night because I was so busy trying to go see Rue and forgot all about it. Hopefully this quiz isn't worth a big percentage of our grade.

"What's up, Truth?" I look up, and I notice Zeke Evans standing in front of me.

Zeke is the last person I want to talk to right now. When I first started school at KHS, he was the first guy I gave my number to. He had the most beautiful dark skin I had ever seen, and he'd make me melt whenever he showed his perfectly white teeth. We texted 24/7, and when we weren't texting we were talking on the phone. Everything changed when some girl from some other school in Atlanta posted a picture of the two of them all hugged up with the caption "#MCM", which means Man Crush Monday. After that, I knew

I couldn't trust him. I cut him off, and ever since then I've been playing guys left and right. He messed everything up for all of them.

"Nothing, Zeke," I respond. "What do you want?"

"I just want to talk." He sits down beside me.

"About what? I'm not in the mood for your mess today."

"About us."

"Excuse me?" I'm stunned. "There's no us. You messed that up for yourself."

"Not really." He laughs, but I don't see anything funny. "You never gave me a chance to explain myself about that little situation from way back when."

"Well, explain then if you must."

"The girl, Kesha, was my ex."

"Was your ex?" I raise my brow. "Is she not your ex anymore?"

"I mean she is my ex," Zeke corrects himself. "Kesha is my ex."

"Ok? Where are you going with this?"

"I just don't want there to be any bad blood between us," he says. "I really liked you, and I think you're a pretty cool girl."

"Why thank you!" I give him fake excitement. "I know I am."

"Stop with the sarcasm," Zeke responds. "I'm serious."

"I bet you are." I roll my eyes.

After a long silence, Zeke continues, "I think we would've been better friends than boyfriend and girlfriend."

"That's the smartest thing I've ever heard you say," I reply. I think the two of us are too much alike to be a couple, but we probably could've been really good friends.

"Do you think we can start over as just friends?" Zeke asks, nervously rubbing the back of his head.

After thinking about it for a second, I reluctantly reply, "Yeah, we can be friends."

"Good!" Zeke smiles.

As soon as I halfway smile back, someone interrupts us saying, "Hey, Truth."

"Hey, what's up?" I respond. It's Nehemiah's fine self.

"How are you doing?" He shakes my hand.

Before I can answer, Zeke interrupts us with one of those fake coughs you give when you're being ignored by someone.

"My apologies, man," Nehemiah says. "What's up?"

"So it's like that now, Christian?" Zeke responds, thinking Nehemiah is Christian.

"I'm not Christian."

"Yes, you are," Zeke says. "We have second period together."

"I'm his twin," Nehemiah informs him. "I'm Nehemiah."

"Seriously?" Zeke asks. "He has a twin?"

"Yes," Nehemiah says. "I just moved back here though."

"Aw ok. I'm Zeke Evans."

"I'm Nehemiah Carter. Nice to meet you, man."

"Do you hoop too?" Zeke asks. Nehemiah is so tall that it's obvious that he plays basketball.

"Yes, I play," Nehemiah answers. "I'm really looking forward to the start of the season."

"Me too," Zeke responds.

"Our first home game is only a few months away," Nehemiah says, looking at me.

Noticing Nehemiah staring at me, Zeke throws shade saying, "I was talking about football season."

After nudging Zeke in his ribs, I say, "Well, I'm looking forward to football and basketball. Our squad is gonna be lit this year!"

"I can't wait to see." Nehemiah grins. "Anyways, the real reason I came over here was to see if you wanted to get together and study sometime. I was gonna text you, but I figured it was better to ask in person."

"Study what?" I ask, knowing I need some help staying on top of my grades since I'm in these advanced classes now.

"How about AP World History?" Nehemiah offers. "I bet that pop quiz threw a curveball at everybody today."

"You're right," I respond. "I didn't even know you were in that class."

"Yeah, I was sitting in the back. I'm kinda shy," Nehemiah says.

"You could've fooled me." I smile.

Nehemiah smiles back. "So, what do you say? Do you want to study together sometime?"

"Let's do it," I say.

"What about me?" Zeke asks. I punch him because I know all he wants is a little attention.

"You can join us too," Nehemiah says.

"Seriously?" Zeke asks, clearly stunned that Nehemiah actually invited him to tag along.

"Yeah," Nehemiah says. "Why not?"

"I was joking, but I guess I could help y'all out a little bit," Zeke says, laughing.

"Are you even in that class?" I ask. Zeke is pretty smart though. He's one of the smartest boys in our school, even as a jock.

"Yeah, I have it third period," Zeke responds.

"With Mrs. Darnell?" I ask.

"Yep," Zeke says.

"I thought that class was only offered during fourth period," I say.

"Nope. There's a class third and fourth period," Zeke responds.

Seconds later, the bell rings, signaling that it's time to head to our next classes.

"I'll catch up with y'all later," Nehemiah says.

"Sounds good." I wave goodbye.

Nehemiah is so dang fine. I'd be all over him if I wasn't trying to figure out where Rue and I were going.

Turning to Zeke, I say, "Bye to you too," before walking away to my 5th period class.

The rest of the day went by smoothly. We didn't do anything in my last couple of classes besides take notes, and cheer practice was short since we only went over a couple of cheers and our halftime performance for tomorrow's football game. I'm so excited to be looking cute in my cheer uniform again.

I'm sitting in the bleachers studying my notes from class and waiting for Micah's practice to end. Then, my moment alone is cut short by a voice I still don't want to hear.

"Truth?" Mercy tries to get my attention.

"What, Mercy?" I roll my eyes.

"I know you're still mad at me," she says. "But we have to go get my car from Rue's house. Remember?" I forgot all about that.

"Yeah," I lie.

"Ryann's cousin said that she could give us a ride."

"Ariana?" I ask, surprised she's even free right now. Because of her lifestyle it's hard to catch her sometimes. She's one of the most infamous strippers in Atlanta.

"Yes, she's already in the parking lot waiting," Mercy says.

"Alright," I say, gathering my things.

"You can text Micah and Love and say you're riding with me."

"I got this!" I raise my voice. "Worry about yourself."

During the whole walk to Ariana's car, Mercy remains silent. I'm glad she does too. I know she's my best friend, but I still can't understand how she could be stupid enough to mess around with a guy that she doesn't even know.

"Hi, Truth," Ariana greets me when I make it to her car.

"What's up, Ariana?" I respond, checking out her BMW coupe that is obviously brand new.

"Nothing much," she answers. "I'm just living life."

"I'm feeling this car though," I let her know.

"I just got it last weekend," she says. "This guy I've been dealing with bought it for me as a gift."

"Cool," I say, wondering who this guy is but I don't want to pry too much.

"So exactly where are we going?" Ariana asks, glancing at Mercy.

"What's the address again, Truth?"

Looking in my phone for the address, I find it and say, "52 Cherokee Rose Cove."

I also text Rue to know we're on the way.

Truth: Sorry for the late notice, but we're on the way to get Mercy's car.

Rue: I'll be here.

I'm glad he texted back because I would hate for us to get there and not be able to get in the gate.

"Do you know where it is?" I ask Ariana, noticing that she hasn't pulled up any GPS.

"Yeah, I know exactly where it is," Ariana responds. "My man lives there."

"Young Rue is your man?" Mercy asks as I sit in the backseat lost for words.

Blushing, Ariana says, "Yeah, he's my man. He's been my man for a good minute now."

Mercy and I both say nothing on the rest of the ride to Rue's crib. I don't even know what to think right now. I thought Rue and I had some potential, and he definitely hasn't been acting like a taken man. I guess he's a dog just like the rest of these dudes. I should've known better than to think he would fall for a fifteen-year-old like me when he probably has thousands of grown women throwing themselves at him.

When we make it to Rue's place, Ariana parks beside Mercy's car. Rue is already standing outside his door.

Slowly exiting Ariana's car, my whole body becomes tense. I don't know whether to be mad, disappointed, or glad I found out about Rue's trifling behind sooner rather than later.

"Hey baby." Rue greets Ariana with a peck on the lips. He has some nerve kissing this girl in front of me when he was all over me last night.

"What's up, boo?" Ariana asks. "Why is my cousin's friend's car at your house?"

"The boys had a little kickback last night," Rue answers. "That was it."

Mercy and I just give each other a look, both noticing how easily this dude just lied.

"Thanks for driving us over here, Ari," Mercy says. "Thanks for letting me keep my car here, Rue."

"You're welcome," Ariana says. "Anything for my cousin's friends!"

"It was no problem," Rue says, not even looking fazed by this messed up situation.

"Well, we're about to get out of here." Mercy heads toward the driver's side of her car as I head to the passenger's side. "Thanks again."

"Ok, see you girls later." Ariana smiles, wrapped in Rue's arms now.

As soon as we're inside Mercy's car, I scream, "Get me out of here. Now!"

I guess this is the thanks I get for falling for a guy that's rich and famous and expecting him to be different simply because he's rich and famous. I can't trust him or anybody else.

~7~

Looking Forward

"Look straight ahead, and fix your eyes on what lies before you."

Proverbs 4:25 NLT

Love

This week has gone well, and it's finally Friday evening. I'm about a week or so ahead on all of my schoolwork, so I can relax for a little bit and focus on other things. With our first football game being tonight and me and Truth's double-date with Christian and Nehemiah being Saturday, I feel like I have a lot to look forward to this weekend.

"Are you ready to go?" Truth says after exiting the school building.

"Yeah, I'm ready," I respond. "Who's driving us?"

"Micah. Duh."

"What's the attitude for now?"

"I don't have an attitude," Truth responds, speeding toward the parking lot now.

"Yes you do." I rush to catch up with her. "As a matter of fact, you've had one since yesterday."

"Love, it's nothing!"

"If it's nothing, why are you being so defensive?"

"Look, Love. I really don't want to talk about this right now." Truth stops in her place. "But if you must know, it's about Rue."

"What about him?" I raise my brow. "I already know about what happened at his place Wednesday night."

"How do you always find out stuff?" she asks, looking annoyed.

"Don't I always tell you that I sense when you're up to something?"

"Maybe I'll start believing you one day," Truth says.

"You really should," I say. "So, what all happened? Mercy told us some of the story, but she didn't tell everything."

"She told you some of the story, huh?" she says. "I bet she didn't tell y'all how she made a fool of herself."

"Yeah, she actually did tell us that," I reply. "She also told us how Rue made a fool of you, too."

"Wow. Thanks a lot, Love." Truth begins to walk off again, visibly hurt. My words might have sounded harsher than I intended them to be.

"Wait up!" I run behind my sister.

By the time I catch up with her, she is already at Micah's car.

"Are you girls ready?" Micah asks, making it to his car shortly after I do.

"Yes," I answer. Truth doesn't say a word.

"We can't stay out too long though," Micah says. "I have to be back at the field house at five o'clock. Do y'all have everything y'all need for tonight?"

"I do," I reply. On gamedays our cheer team is allowed to wear our cheer uniforms to school. I keep everything else I need, like my cheer shoes and water bottle, in my cheer duffle bag.

"What about you, Truth?" Micah looks in his rearview mirror at Truth.

"Yeah," she says, rolling her eyes.

"What's wrong with her today?" Micah asks me.

"Boy drama."

"Boy drama?" Micah scrunches up his face. "With who?"

"Nobody," I lie.

"That's not a good look on you, Love." Micah shakes his head.

"What do you mean?"

"Lying," Micah answers. "You know you don't lie."

"It just isn't my business to tell," I reply.

"I see," Micah says. "So, how was your first week back?"

"It actually went pretty well," I respond. "I'm ahead in all of my classes, and it was fun getting back into cheerleading. I'm just trying to make sure I stay focused on my relationship with God despite everything that's going on."

"Everything like what?" Micah asks.

I want to tell him about my nonstop feelings about Christian, but I don't feel comfortable talking to my brother about boys. He might try to shut it down before it even begins. However, I can tell he really likes Christian, so it might be different.

"Just everything," I reply, ready to change the subject. "How was your first week? It's hard believing you're a senior."

"It was decent," Micah says. "I've been waiting for this moment forever."

"It's a blessing, huh?" I smile. I'm so proud of Micah. A lot of black males aren't able to say they're so close to getting a diploma for various reasons, but my brother made it. He's not out here gang-banging, doing drugs, or getting girls pregnant, but he's focused on school, football, and furthering his relationship with God. I love it!

"You know it!" Micah smacks the steering wheel.

"What's the best part of being a senior?"

"Good question," he comments. "I think the best part might be just being so close to your dreams coming true. You know what I mean?"

"I think so."

"That was kinda vague." Micah laughs. "You know I'm trying to play football on the next level, and that has always been one of my biggest dreams."

"Yeah, I know."

"I'm so close to it now that it's scary."

"Why is it scary?" I ask.

"The uncertainty of all of it is what's scary," Micah responds. "I don't know which college God is leading me to yet."

"How do you think you'll know which one is the one for you?"

"When the time is right, God is going to make it clear to me. I just know He is."

"Well, just know that no matter where you go I'm so proud of you."

"I appreciate it." Micah smiles. "I have to set the bar high for you and Truth. I want y'all to know that y'all can do whatever y'all are willing to pray and work hard for."

Breaking her silence, Truth says, "Can we go to Marta's Garden?"

"Yeah, that's where I was headed," Micah answers.

Marta's Garden is one of our favorite places to eat in Atlanta. It's a vegetarian restaurant, but it is known to be inhabited by both vegetarians and non-vegetarians because the food is so delicious.

"Trying to eat healthy before the game, huh?" I playfully remark.

"That's always." Micah flashes a big smile. "You know I have to have my body right in order to stay on top of my game."

"Whatever you say, big bro."

Two minutes into the game, we've already added a touchdown to the scoreboard. Micah threw the ball 52 yards to Joel for a beautiful touchdown, and the extra point attempt was good. Now, we're back on the offensive end of the ball again.

"Let's go, 88!" Mercy cheers for Joel. Mercy is the perfect cheerleader girlfriend. Every time Joel does anything she cheers, even if it's not so good. She even has his number written in face paint on each one of her cheeks. Maybe Truth and I should do that for Micah.

"Here we go, Panthers!" I chant towards the crowd as our team rushes for another first down.

Friday night football is a big deal in the South. The stadium is so packed that it looks like a NFL game instead of a high school game, and I feel like I'm feeding off of the energy that I'm receiving from the crowd. Although I'm usually shy and quiet, it's a different story when I'm on the sidelines cheering. Cheerleading is one of my passions, so I come completely out of my shell when I'm performing.

My parents are sitting in the section directly in front of the cheerleaders along with some of our family members from Arkansas who traveled to see this game. I'm so happy that our favorite cousins, Evan and Eva, were able to come down. They're all dressed in our school colors, which are blue, black, and silver.

Evan is the same age as Micah, and Eva is the same age as Truth and me. Evan is a 6'11 senior and is being heavily recruited by some of the top schools in the nation for basketball, like Duke, Kentucky, and Arkansas, and Eva is following in his footsteps. She's six feet tall and also a great basketball player.

"Look, Love." Mercy waves one of her pompoms to the left side of the crowd.

As if it is fate or something, Christian and I lock eyes. I smile and wave my pompoms in his direction, and he smiles and waves back.

As soon as my dad sees Christian, his face lights up and he flags him over.

I obviously can't hear what is being said, but it looks like my dad is introducing Christian to my whole family. Then, Christian takes a seat on the end of the row next to Eva and begins talking to her.

I'm not feeling jealous or anything, but I know Eva is beautiful. I'll just have to make sure I tell her Christian is off-limits.

“And there goes Micah Hudson for another Panthers touchdown!” The announcer booms through the speakers. The crowd erupts in applause and screams, and our cheer team begins to do the dance we do to our fight song, which is being played by our marching band right now.

The Panthers have taken an early 14-0 lead. If this is any indicator of how the rest of this game is going to go, this is going to be an exciting first football game of the season.

After the game ends in a 56-0 victory, the fans rush onto the field. With the way that everyone is acting, you would have suspected that we just won a national championship. Nevertheless, this is a great feeling.

“Way to go, big bro,” I congratulate Micah as I spot him in the center of the field.

“Thanks, Love,” Micah says, embracing me in a tight hug.

“You did your thing!” Truth screams, rushing toward us.

“What did you expect?” Micah laughs, bringing Truth in for a hug as well.

“Ew! You stink,” Truth says, pinching her nose.

“So!” Micah replies. “Let’s go find our people.”

As we get close to the sidelines, we spot our parents and the rest of our family.

“I’m so proud of you, son.” Dad hugs Micah.

"I bet Arkansas can't wait to have you," Uncle Mike, Evan and Eva's dad, chimes in.

"Wait a minute now, Mike," my mama interrupts. "He hasn't made a decision yet."

"Boy, what are you waiting for?" Uncle Mike asks, nudging Micah in his ribs.

"I'll make a decision soon, Unc," Micah replies. "I'm just glad y'all could make it out here."

"We wouldn't have missed it for the world," Evan says, shaking Micah's hand.

"Thanks fam," Micah responds.

Micah and Evan have been close to each other since as long as I can remember. You could hardly ever see one of them without the other being somewhere nearby. I know Evan was upset when our family decided to move to Atlanta, but I'm glad the move didn't place a strain on their relationship.

"Guess who," a voice coming from behind Micah interrupts. Judging by the small arms I see wrapped around Micah's waist, I know it's Joy.

Turning around, Micah greets Joy with a kiss on the forehead.

"All that hard work and prayer is paying off," Joy says. "You played so well tonight!"

"Thanks, sweetie," Micah replies. "Meet my family, Joy."

"Wow, she's a pretty one," Aunt Tina says.

"Thank you," Joy says, blushing.

"Joy, this is Uncle Mike, Aunt Tina, their son Evan, and their daughter Eva," Micah introduces them. "This is Joy, y'all. She's my girlfriend."

"It's so nice to finally meet you all!" Joy smiles and hugs each of them one by one.

"Well, I cooked a big meal tonight, and you're welcome to join us," Mama says to Joy.

"Thank you, Mrs. Hudson," Joy replies. "I'd love to join."

"You can invite Mercy over too," Mama offers.

"Thanks again, Mrs. Hudson, but I think Mercy already has plans for tonight," Joy says.

"Umm, about that..." Truth interrupts. "I was wondering if I could go out tonight, too."

"Go out where?" Mama asks.

"Some of our friends are throwing a small party—"

"Absolutely not," Mama cuts Truth off.

"But why not?" Truth counters.

"Excuse me?" Mama cocks her head to the side and puts her hands on her hips. Our mom, Laila Bryant-Hudson, is a sweet as can be, but if she feels disrespected, she can be ruthless. She's obviously stunned that Truth had the nerve to ask her for an explanation.

"Nevermind," Truth responds.

"That's what I thought," Mama says.

"You'll be alright, Truth," Micah says to her. "Have some fun with us tonight."

"Whatever," Truth says under her breath.

When we get home, I'm surprised to see all of the decorations adorning our house along with the big feast that my mama has prepared. She has all of our favorites. There's chicken spaghetti, collard greens, corn on the cob, macaroni and cheese, sweet potato pie, and so much more.

"Wow, honey." Daddy takes his place at the head of the table. "You've really outdone yourself this time."

"Thanks," Mama replies. "I try." My mama is so talented in everything she does, and I admire how humble she is about it all. She's one of the most prominent lawyers in the South, but she still manages to take care of the home and lead a healthy spiritual life.

"Everyone make yourselves at home," Daddy says.

"Mrs. Hudson, your decorations look amazing," Joy says as she settles into the seat Micah has pulled out for her.

"And it's smelling good in here, too!" Micah adds.

"Thanks, sweethearts," Mama responds.

The house is decorated with a football theme. The centerpiece in the table has been crafted with paper footballs and artificial grass. Random pictures of Micah are also strategically placed throughout the dining room.

"This home is gorgeous," Aunt Tina compliments. "Do y'all like it better than the one y'all had back in Arkansas?"

"It's definitely more spacious, but I really do miss the lake that we had out back," Mama replies.

"Me too," I agree. "I loved doing my homework while sitting by the lake."

"I remember that one time the wind blew your homework into the lake." Eva laughs.

"I forgot all about that!" I reply. "Mrs. Thorn tried to give me an F because she didn't believe me."

Suddenly, our doorbell rings.

"Who is that?" Truth says with an attitude.

"I'll get that." Daddy rushes out of his seat to the front door.

Shortly after, he comes back into the dining room with two other people.

"Hey, it's good to see y'all again." Christian walks into the room with a big smile on his face. "Thanks for inviting us Pastor Hudson."

"We appreciate it," Nehemiah adds, grabbing a seat near Truth.

"It's my pleasure." Daddy returns to his seat. "Now let's say grace and eat."

"Finally." Micah claps and laughs. "I've been waiting on this meal since before my game started."

Everyone else begins to laugh at Micah before bowing their heads and closing their eyes to allow my father to bless our food.

After dinner, Micah, Truth, Joy, Eva, Evan, Nehemiah, Christian, and I gather in the backyard to chill, talk, and vibe to some good music.

"How does it feel, Micah?" Evan asks Micah as the song on the playlist switches.

"How does what feel?" Micah responds.

"How does it feel to know that you're literally the man here in Atlanta?"

"I wouldn't say I'm the man, but I do know I'm blessed. I'm living my dream here."

"So where do you think you're going to go to school?" Eva asks.

"At this point, I'm not really sure," Micah answers. "I'd love to play in the south, but I'll go to whichever school gives me the best offer."

"Do you think you would come back and play for Arkansas?" Eva asks.

"Yeah, I love U of A," Micah replies.

"How do you feel about that, Joy?" Eva asks.

"How do I feel about what?" Joy responds.

"How do you feel about Micah possibly going back to Arkansas?"

"I just want what God wants for him," Joy replies. "If he's meant to go and play for Arkansas, then I'll be fine with him going to do that."

"Would you follow him?" Eva asks.

Without hesitation, Joy says, "No, I wouldn't go to Arkansas just to follow him."

"What do you mean?" Truth jumps into the conversation. "Don't you love him?"

"Of course I love him, but I wouldn't go to Arkansas just to follow him. I have dreams of my own, and I want to go to the college that's right for me. If it's Arkansas, or anywhere that Micah decides to go, then that's great. However, if it's not the same college that Micah decides to go to, I'm sure we'll be alright."

"Dang," Evan says. "What do you have to say about that, man?"

Micah says, "That's fine with me."

"Really?" Evan asks. "You don't wanna have your girl near you?"

"Yeah, I wanna have Joy near me, but I respect her and her dreams too," Micah says. "If we're not at the same school, I'm sure we could still make things work between us."

"Aren't you scared other girls might try to go after him?" I ask. I feel like insecurity within a relationship may be my biggest issue when I get into a relationship, so I want to hear what Joy has to say about this.

"Honestly, I don't trust other girls around my man," Joy says. "But I do trust my man around other girls."

"I wish we could say that about some of these other dudes out here," Truth says.

"Not every guy is the same," Nehemiah says.

"I wasn't saying that every guy is the same," Truth snaps back. "I'm just saying that not every guy can be trusted."

"You just have to find one worth putting your trust in," Joy adds, rubbing Micah's hand.

"I have yet to find a guy that I can fully trust," Truth says. "That's why I can't commit to these dudes."

"Well, maybe you're trying to put your trust in the wrong type of dudes," Nehemiah responds to Truth again.

"How do you know the type of dudes I'm trying to put my trust in?" Truth raises her voice. "Boy, you don't even know me!"

"Calm down, sis," Micah intervenes. "He's probably talking about the Young Rue situation."

"And how would he know about that?" Truth counters.

"I was around when Mercy was talking about it," Nehemiah says.

"None of y'all know the whole situation, so don't speak on it." Truth rolls her eyes.

"What Young Rue situation?" Eva asks. "Are you talking about Young Rue the rapper?"

"Yeah," Micah replies. "I wasn't going to bring it up to you, Truth, because I figured you learned your lesson."

"What happened?" Evan asks.

For a long time, no one says anything. Christian and I look at each other like we can't believe this is happening right now. Everyone else is looking at Truth, waiting for her to give us a rundown of how everything went down.

When it's clear that Truth isn't going to say anything about what happened that night, Nehemiah says, "You're worth so much more than that, Truth."

Although the lights are dim in the backyard, I notice a small tear fall down Truth's face as she abruptly gets up to go back inside the house.

I can tell that she is hurt by the way that things went down with Young Rue, but what did she expect to happen? He's a rapper, and he probably hasn't even accepted God into his life. He probably plays girls like this for a living. I just hate that this had to happen to my sister.

"Did I say something wrong?" Nehemiah looks confused.

"She's just hurting right now, man," Micah answers. "She'll be fine. I'll make sure of that."

"Bro, she'll appreciate what you said later," Christian says.

"I'm so lost right now," Eva says. "Do Truth and Young Rue know each other or something?"

"You'll have to talk to her about that when she's ready to talk about it," I say, trying to protect my sister's right to privacy. "Let's just chill and enjoy the rest of our night."

~8~

Double Date

"Guard your heart above all else, for it determines the course of your life."
Proverbs 4:23 NLT

Truth

I want to be mad at Nehemiah for what he said to me last night, but I have no reason to be mad. I can't even be mad at Rue. I can only be mad at myself for allowing myself to let my guard down for a guy like him. Maybe I do put my trust in the wrong type of dudes.

Although it's the weekend, I just want to stay in my room all day. I don't feel like going anywhere, but me and Love's double date with Christian and Nehemiah is today. Any other time, I would have been excited about our parents letting us go on our first official date, especially with a pair of fine dudes like Christian and Nehemiah. With the way everything has gone down this week, I have no desire to go out with Nehemiah or anyone else.

While I am in mid thought, I hear a soft knock at my door.

“Who is it?” I yell toward the door.

“It’s me,” Love responds. “Can I come in?”

“Yeah,” I say, putting my phone down. For the past few hours, I have been scrolling through Rue’s Instagram page and wishing things could have worked out differently. I was beginning to like the idea of possibly becoming his girl. It should have been us. It could have been us.

“Christian said they should be here in about twenty minutes,” Love says, taking a seat on my windowsill. “How are you feeling?”

“I’m alright,” I say, trying to hide my true feelings.

“How do you really feel?” Love asks. “Tell the truth, Truth.”

“I feel like crap, and I really don’t want to go on this date.” I put air quotes around the word “date”.

“Why not? Is it because of what Nehemiah said last night?”

“It’s that and a combination of everything else that happened this week. I’m just not feeling it.”

“Do you want me to call them and cancel? We can if you really want to, Truth.”

“No, you don’t have to do all that.”

Love is seriously crushing on Christian, and Christian is crushing back. This is a first for her, and I don't want to be the one to ruin it for her. Usually I'm ok with being selfish, but not this time.

"Are you sure?" Love joins me on my bed.

"Yeah, I'm sure."

"Good because I'm excited but nervous at the same time," Love admits.

"Why are you nervous?" I ask. "You already know Christian likes you."

"How do I know that?" Love asks, skeptically.

"Are you serious?" I laugh. "He's always trying to be around you, and he's already trying to get in good with the family. He definitely likes you, girl."

"I just thought he was being friendly or something."

"Quit playing." I roll my eyes. "You know that boy likes you."

Laughing, Love says, "Well, yeah I kinda knew that, but for some reason I just find it hard to believe. He's literally so perfect for me that it's scary."

"Just don't fall too fast or you'll end up like me."

"I won't," Love replies. "I'm going to make sure I'm seeking God the whole way, so I don't get too caught up in my feelings. You know?"

"I see what you're saying," I say.

Maybe I need to start messing around with more Christian guys instead of these wannabe bad boys and playboys. Maybe I wouldn't get let down so much.

"What time is it?" Love says reaching for my cell before I can stop her.

She instantly notices that I've been scrolling through Rue's pictures because I didn't exit Instagram when I sat my phone down.

"Why is this the first thing that pops up?" Love turns my phone around to show me one of Rue's pictures.

"I don't know," I lie.

"Stop lying, Truth. Is this what you were sitting in here doing all morning?"

"I haven't even been up all morning, so no." I try to get out of fully telling the truth.

"I hope you know this isn't healthy for you," Love says. "You can't be sitting up here reminiscing about this dude after the way he treated you."

"You think I don't know that?" I say with an attitude. "Let's just leave it alone.

"Alright." Love puts her hands up in surrender. "Hopefully after today, you'll be thinking about someone else."

"Who?" I ask.

Love fake coughs and says, "Nehemiah."

"Girl, quit playing," I reply. "You need to get out so I can finish getting ready."

"You look ready to me," Love responds.

"Well I'm not, so get out." I toss a pillow at her.

"Fine!" Love laughs. "I'll be downstairs waiting on you. Don't take all day getting ready either."

"You know me." I wink.

When I make it downstairs, I notice my daddy, mama, sister, and brother all sitting in the living room.

"Dang, is this really that big of a deal?" I sarcastically remark as I take a seat next to Micah.

"Of course," Daddy says. "It's my baby girls' first outing with some young fellas, and I wouldn't miss it for the world."

"Sure Daddy." I laugh.

Glancing around the room, I see my mama giving me this weird look.

"Why are you looking at me like that?" I ask her.

"Don't you think you should have dressed more modestly?" Mama responds.

"What's wrong with what I have on?" I ask, confused. I have on some dark, skinny leg jeans and a black, off-the-shoulder top with some black thigh high boots.

"Did you look in the mirror?" Mama says.

"Um, yeah."

"Well, you should've seen the problem. Go upstairs and change before the boys get here," Mama replies.

"Is there something wrong with me showing my shoulders?" I ask, annoyed.

"Go do as I said," she replies, raising her voice. "Your breasts are just about hanging out of that shirt."

"Whatever," I mutter under my breath as I head back upstairs to change.

I bet if Love had on this outfit, my mama wouldn't have made her change. I swear it feels like she likes Love more than me sometimes. Love can do whatever she pleases, but there's always a problem when I try to do me.

When I make it back to my room, I frantically search my closet for something else to wear. Although I no longer wanted to go on this date, I put a lot of thought into the outfit I have on now.

Suddenly my phone rings, and I see it's Ava calling.

"What's up, Ava?" I answer the phone.

"Truth, what you doing?"

"Finding something to wear for this double date with Christian and Nehemiah."

"Why you not already dressed?" Ava asks.

"I was dressed, but that mother of mine is making me change."

"Change because what?"

"She says my boobs are popping out of my shirt." I roll my eyes.

"So? Just put a jacket on, and she no see them," Ava says. "That's what I do." I know I probably shouldn't do that, but it's a great idea considering how crunched for time I am.

"I think that's what I'm about to do," I respond, closing my closet door after grabbing a black, leather jacket. "Thanks."

"You welcome," Ava replies. "You like Nehemiah, right? He look so good."

"He does look good, but I don't like him or anyone else right now. I'm so tired of these dudes."

"That's why I don't give them time. They play too much," Ava says. "But I let you go now. Have fun."

"Thanks, girl," I say. "I'll call you back later."

"Ok bye," Ava responds, hanging up the phone.

As I'm about to walk out of my room, my cell rings again. This time it's a Facetime call from Zeke.

As soon as the Facetime call connects, I say, "What do you want, Zeke? I'm busy."

"Dang, that's rude," Zeke responds. "Is that how you're supposed to talk to your best friend?"

"Best friend is an overstatement," I respond. "I agreed to be your friend. That's it."

"Sure." Zeke smiles. "Where do you think you're going?"

"I'm going out with my sister, Christian, and Nehemiah."

"For what?" Zeke asks.

"Dang, you're so nosey!"

"I'm your friend, so you should tell me these types of things. Are y'all going on a date or something?"

"Or something." I roll my eyes. "Now what do you want?"

"I just wanted to see how you're doing. That's it."

"How do I look like I'm doing?" I snap. "I really don't have time to be talking to you right now."

"Well, I'll call you back later then."

"Yeah ok," I say, hitting the end call button.

Zeke's feelings look like they were hurt, but oh well. I guess we're even.

"Hurry up girl!" I hear Micah shout as I inch closer to the stairs.

"I'm coming!" I shout back, beginning to walk down the stairs.

As soon as I make it down the stairs, I spot Nehemiah standing at the edge of the stairs with a bouquet of red roses in his hands.

"These are for you, Truth." Nehemiah extends the roses to me.

"Thanks," I say, grabbing the roses and continuing to walk past him. "Are y'all ready?"

"Yes, let's go." Christian smiles at Love. I notice Love also has a bouquet of roses in her hands. Her roses are pink instead of red though.

"Should we get a picture before y'all go?" my dad asks.

"No, Daddy. That's too much," I respond. He's so embarrassing.

"Are you sure?" Daddy replies.

"I don't mind," Nehemiah says.

"Let's do it," Christian adds.

"Take it in front of the fireplace," Mama says. "The background will look nice."

As soon as we're all lined in front of the fireplace, my dad says, "Squeeze in a little tighter. The boys aren't all the way in."

Christian and Nehemiah are on the ends, and Love and I are in the middle. As Nehemiah moves in more, he places one hand on the small of my back. This sends shivers down my spine. I felt something similar when I was with Rue, but this is something stronger.

As soon as we take the picture, I'm the first one out of the door. I need to put as much distance between me and Nehemiah as possible.

"Y'all have fun!" Daddy yells after us.

"And be careful with my sisters!" Micah adds.

"I'm driving, so Love you can sit up front with me," Christian says. "Truth you can sit in the backseat with Nehemiah if you don't mind."

"I don't mind." I roll my eyes. So much for putting distance between me and him. "Where are we going anyways?"

"It's a surprise." Christian grins.

"I'm excited," Love says as Christian opens the car door for her.

"We are too," Nehemiah says as he opens the door for me.

When we make it to our destination, I'm a little surprised. We're at The Panther Den, our high school's basketball arena.

"Why are we here?" I ask.

"This is the first part of our date," Nehemiah answers.

"What kind of date is this?" I turn up my nose. I'm too cute to be sitting up in some smelly gym.

"You'll enjoy it," Nehemiah says. "Now, come on."

Once we're on the gym floor, I notice four seats with basketball jerseys, shorts, and shoes on them.

"To start things off, we thought it would be a little fun to play a game of two on two basketball," Christian says.

"Me and Truth against you and Nehemiah?" Love asks.

"That wouldn't be fair," Christian says. "It's going to be me and you versus Nehemiah and Truth."

"I have no idea how to play basketball," Love admits.

"I don't either," I say, crossing my arms across my chest.

"That's fine," Christian says. "We're just here to have some fun."

"Just try your best." Nehemiah rubs my shoulder. I look at him as if to say "don't touch me", and he removes his hand.

"First, let's change into the proper attire." Christian leads us to the seats where the jerseys and stuff are. "Love and I are wearing pink. Y'all are wearing purple."

"Why pink, bro?" Nehemiah asks, laughing uncontrollably.

"Man, it was one of the only options they had since it was so last minute." Christian slaps Nehemiah on the arm.

"Whatever you say." Nehemiah continues laughing.

"Love looks beautiful in pink anyways," Christian compliments my sister.

"Aww, thanks!" Love blushes.

"You're welcome." Christian blushes too. "Nehemiah, where is our referee?"

"He's on the way," Nehemiah says.

"No he isn't," a loud voice interrupts. "He's here."

It's Zeke. Oh Lord.

"Why is your ex our referee?" Love whispers in my ear, unable to contain her laughter.

"He claims I'm his best friend now," I say, shaking my head. "It's weird, but it might work."

"Y'all are too much alike," Love says.

"That's the same thing I was thinking."

"Surprise, surprise." Zeke walks over and hugs me and Love.

"Why didn't you tell me you were coming when we were on the phone?" I shove him.

"Because it was a surprise."

"Whatever."

"Since he told me he was your best friend, I asked him to come here for moral support," Nehemiah says.

"He's not—"

"And I most graciously said yes," Zeke says with a cheesy smile on his face, interrupting me before I could get the words out of my mouth.

"What do you need moral support for anyways?" I ask Nehemiah.

"Just in case you try to kill me with a basketball or something," Nehemiah says. "You know anything could happen."

"I don't hate you that much."

"You sure?" he asks.

"Positive," I reply.

It's weird thinking about how much I was attracted to Nehemiah in the beginning and how excited I was when he asked me to study with him. Now I feel so guarded, and I can't help it. I guess the truth that he was spitting to me last night hurt me in a way I can't explain.

"Are y'all done talking?" Christian asks. "Or are y'all just trying to avoid this butt whooping me and Love are about to put on y'all?"

"We'll see about that," Nehemiah responds. "Let's just get dressed, so we can get this thing started."

"Loser pays for lunch," Christian says.

"Bet." Nehemiah shakes Christian's hand.

Two hours later, Christian, Nehemiah, Love, and I are sitting in a booth at Daisy's Diner. Christian and Love won the bet.

"I'll be sure to order the most expensive thing since I know you're paying," Christian gloats.

"Next time we'll win," Nehemiah says. "Ain't that right, Truth?"

"Whatever," I say and return to looking at the menu.

I fell while we were playing basketball and bruised my knee. I'm ready to eat and go home. I never wanted to play the stupid game anyway.

"How can I help you?" a familiar voice asks.

When I look up, I notice Ryann is standing there in an apron with a pen and pad in her hand.

"What are you doing here?" I ask.

"I work here now," Ryann says, looking at her shoes. "I meant to tell y'all, but we've all been so busy this week." I'm so shocked right now, but I guess Ryann would be the first one who I'd expect to get a job out of our friend group.

"This is Ryann, one of our best friends," Love introduces her. "Ryann, this is Christian and Nehemiah."

"Nice to meet you again, Ryann." Christian shakes her hand. "We met at the basketball mixer last year."

"Oh yeah! I forgot all about that," Ryann says.

“Good afternoon,” Nehemiah says.

“Good afternoon. It’s nice to meet you again.” Ryann shakes Nehemiah’s hand. “You ate lunch with us the other day, right?”

“Yeah, that was me,” he responds.

“How long have you been working here?” I interrupt their friendly greetings.

“I just started today.”

“Oh. Do you like it?”

“It’s a job that pays,” Ryann replies. “So, do y’all know what you want to order?”

“Yes ma’am,” Nehemiah says before placing his order.

After he’s done, everyone else also places their order. I decide to go with the chicken alfredo and a lemonade to drink.

When Ryann walks away, Christian says, “She’s so cold at basketball. I know she’s going pro one day.”

“Really?” Nehemiah asks. “Does she play for the school?”

“Yeah, she started last year as a freshman. She was the main reason they won the championship game.”

“I can’t wait to see her play then.”

“Are y’all going to the scrimmage game next week?” Ryann pops back up at our table.

“What day is it on?” Christian asks.

“It’s Monday after school at 5,” Ryann answers.

"We'll be there then," Christian says. "What about you girls?"

"Anything for Ryann," Love says, smiling at Ryann.

"You too?" Ryann asks me.

"I'll be there," I reply, even though I hate basketball games.

"You promise?"

"Yeah, I promise."

"Good," Ryann says. "I have to get back to work, but your food is gonna be out in a little bit."

"Thanks," Christian and Nehemiah say in unison.

While we're waiting for our food, I decide to social media stalk Nehemiah since I haven't done it already. I have the habit of looking up any guy that is interested in me and vice versa on social media so I can see what type of person they are and if they already have a girl or not.

One of the first pictures I see on his Facebook profile is of him and this blonde girl hugging. The caption says "I hope you're enjoying ATL, Nemo. I miss you so much!"

"So, Nehemiah, do you have a girlfriend?" I blurt out.

"No, why you ask that?" He looks surprised by my question.

"I'm just asking."

"Why are you just asking? I wouldn't be here if I had a girlfriend."

"And why is that?"

"Why do you think?" Nehemiah asks. "I'm sure no girl would be cool with her man being out with another girl."

"So true, man," Christian says.

"You must be scrolling through my Facebook page?" Nehemiah glances over at me.

"No," I lie. "Why would I be doing that? I'm not a stalker."

"Well, I see the Facebook app open on your phone," he says. "And you just all of a sudden became concerned about my relationship status. You must've saw that post from Kelly?"

"Who is Kelly?" Love asks.

"Kelly is a girl that I went to church with in Cali," Nehemiah says. "We used to be leaders for our youth group."

"Sounds cool!" Love says.

"Cali?" I ask.

"Yeah, that's where I used to live last year when our parents divorced."

"Love didn't tell you?" Christian asks.

"No, I didn't," Love says. "I didn't know if it was something you wanted me to talk about. I try to respect people's privacy."

"I respect that." Christian nods.

"See, you're getting jealous for nothing." Nehemiah laughs.

"I wasn't getting jealous. Don't flatter yourself, " I respond.

"You don't have to lie." Nehemiah laughs again. "Next time don't assume, just ask."

"I did ask." I roll my eyes.

"True, true."

"Yeah." I continue scrolling on my phone. Almost all of Nehemiah's posts are about God and sports.

"I think me and Love are going to move over to the next booth so we can talk in private," Christian says. "Is that cool with you, Love?"

"Uh, yeah that's fine," Love says, looking nervous.

Once they've moved to the next booth, Nehemiah says, "Are you ok, Truth?"

"What do you mean?" I place my phone in my lap.

"When we first met, you were so nice to me. Now, it's like you can't even stand to be around me. What changed?"

"Nothing changed."

"Was it last night?" he asks. "I'm sorry about that. I didn't mean to make you upset."

"Last night didn't faze me."

"Well, can you help me understand you better?"

I look into his eyes, and I can tell he's genuinely interested in me. I know I could easily break this guy's heart, but I really don't want to because I now know how it feels to literally have your heart ripped out. He's better off not even falling for me.

Before I get to answer his question, Ryann comes to our table with our food.

"Thanks boo." I smile at her.

"You're welcome." Ryann winks at me.

"Thank you, Ryann," Nehemiah says.

"You're welcome," Ryann responds. "Y'all enjoy the food."

Before taking a bite of his food, Nehemiah takes a long look at me. I think he's trying to see if I'm going to answer his question, but I'm not. I don't have the energy to try to explain all of my confusion to him.

After he gets the hint, he says grace and begins eating his food. Then, my phone vibrates with an unexpected message.

Rue: Truth, we need to talk.

How dare he have the nerve to text me again? After what went down at his house the other day, I don't ever want to see him again. He thought he played me, but truthfully, he played himself. I wonder if I should respond to him though.

"Truth, I know you're not about to respond to that text while you're with me," Nehemiah interrupts my thoughts.

"Huh? What are you talking about?" I ask.

"I'm not stupid or blind," he says. "I saw the message pop up on your phone."

"Why do you keep being so nosey?" I snap at him.

"You know what, Truth? Forget this," Nehemiah says and rises from his seat. "Text him back. I don't care."

"If you wouldn't have been looking at my phone, your feelings wouldn't be hurt now!" I let him have it. I'm so sick of these dudes.

"Christian, I'm leaving," Nehemiah says when he makes it to where Christian and Love are sitting. "I don't care if I have to take the bus, but I have to get out of here. I'm wasting my time, and I don't like being disrespected when I'm trying to do everything right."

"Calm down, bro. What's going on?" Christian asks.

"She'd rather be with Rue right now, and I don't have time for it."

"What do you mean?" Love asks.

"Ask your sister," Nehemiah responds. "She's over there texting him now."

"I hear you over there talking, and I haven't even texted him back yet," I scream across the room.

"Let's just go," Love says, looking embarrassed.

People at the other tables are staring, and I see Ryann coming our way.

"What's going on over here?" Ryann asks. "I can hear y'all all the way in the back."

"Nothing anymore," Nehemiah answers. "I'm ready to pay, Ryann. I'll just leave your tip at the front counter."

"Was something wrong with the food?" Ryann asks.

"No, your friend would just rather be somewhere else."

"Shut the hell up, Nehemiah!" I yell at him.

"Be quiet, Truth, before I get in trouble," Ryann says. "You know it's my first day."

"My bad, girl." I try to calm down. "I'm about to go finish my food."

"Yeah, go do that," Nehemiah responds.

"I wasn't talking to you!" I say as I walk off.

Forget Nehemiah, and forget this date too. I'm about to do whatever I want to do.

As soon as I get back to my seat, I grab my phone to text Rue back.

Truth: Let's talk then.

~9~

What You Wanna Do?

"Don't act thoughtlessly, but understand what the Lord wants you to do."
Ephesians 5:17 NLT

Love

"Mercy, I can't believe Truth acted the way she did today," I say into my phone.

"What did she do?" Mercy asks.

"She was so rude to Nehemiah on our date," I respond. "Then, all of a sudden, Nehemiah leaves because he said he can't take it anymore. I was so embarrassed!"

"What was she doing?"

"He said she was texting Rue while they were together."

"Are you serious?" Mercy asks. "That can't be true."

"Well, that's what he said."

"Have you asked her about it though?"

"No," I respond. "She won't even say a word to me. You know how she gets when she's mad."

"Yeah, I know," Mercy says. "We really haven't talked since the incident at Rue's place."

"Really? She hasn't said a word to you?"

"Not really, but I would be mad at me too."

"We all make mistakes, Mercy. We live, we learn, and we just have to ask God for forgiveness and move forward."

"I know," Mercy replies. "What should we do?"

"I'm just going to give her some space and let her come around whenever she feels like it," I say.

"Good idea," Mercy says. "Do you want to go somewhere with me next month?"

"Next month? What's going on?"

"I wanted to go on a few of Joy's college visits with her, so I can get a feel of what it's going to be like."

"You're already thinking about college, too?" I ask. "I'm glad I'm not the only one who's already thinking about where I want to go."

"Yeah, I am. Plus, it's the only way I can seem to get my parents off my back."

"How are they doing though?"

"They're alright I guess. They're still on my back about Joel."

"How are you and Joel doing?" I ask, curious. Everyone knows about Mercy hanging out with Rue and his friends the other night. Apparently, Joel was really pissed and has been telling the whole school how terrible Mercy is. I don't think she knows though, but I'm not going to be the one to bring it up.

"We actually haven't talked," she responds.

"Do you miss him?"

"Of course I do. He's my everything, Love."

"Do you want me to try to talk to him for you?" I ask. Since my brother and Joel are so close, Joel is like another brother to me.

"Would you really do that for me?" Mercy asks. "I'd appreciate it."

"He's over here now, so I can do it right now if you want." He's been over here for the last few hours playing video games with Micah.

"He's over there?! I'm coming."

"No, you're not," I respond. "Stay where you are and let me handle this."

"Don't start thinking you're a relationship expert because you and Christian are doing so well." Mercy laughs.

"On that note, I'm hanging up." I laugh before clicking the end button. I don't know why I offered to talk to Joel for Mercy, but I don't like not keeping my word.

When I make it to the game room, the boys are still sitting in the same spots as they were before when I came in here. I don't see how they can play these games for hours on end.

"What's up, Love?" Micah notices me creeping into the room.

"I want to play the game," I respond.

"Love, stop. You don't want to play this game. What's up?" Micah asks.

"I just needed to ask Joel something."

"If it's about Mercy, I don't want to hear it." Joel doesn't take his eyes off the television screen.

"Y'all just need to squash this beef and just talk," Micah says.

"I agree," I add.

"Whatever y'all. That girl disrespected me so bad," Joel responds. "Ole dude can have her."

"That girl is still your girlfriend," Micah says. "You need to talk to her."

"You talk to her," Joel replies. "I don't want to talk to her."

I shake my head. "You're so stubborn, Joel."

"Oh well." Joel dismisses the conversation.

"I guess I'll go back to my room," I say.

"To do what?" Micah asks.

"I think I'm about to do some reading."

"Ok cool," he replies before directing his attention back to his game.

When I'm back in my room, I decide to check my email before I start reading. I noticed earlier that I had about ten unread messages. Most of them are spam messages, but I see one from the STEM Society of Atlanta. STEM stands for science, technology, engineering, and mathematics.

Dear Love Hudson, we would like to extend an offer to you to become one of the STEM Society of Atlanta's research assistants. If this sounds like something you would be interested in, please give us a call at 555-870-8787.

I can't believe this! This is a rare blessing. Becoming a research assistant at the STEM Society is very difficult, and I have never heard of a high school student being able to do this. This opportunity would definitely help me in the future because I hope to study biomedical engineering when I get to college.

"Mama!" I yell as I begin running down the stairs.

"Yes, Love?"

"Guess what!"

"What is it?" She raises her head out of the book that she was reading.

"I've just been offered a position as a research assistant for the STEM Society!"

"Praise God!" Daddy interrupts, coming from the dining room.

"Love, that's amazing! Congratulations!" Mama says.

"When do you start, baby?" Daddy asks.

"I'm not sure yet," I respond. "They asked me to give them a call.

“Well, what are you waiting for? Go call them.” Mama smiles.

“They’re closed on the weekends, so I’ll have to do it first thing next week.”

“Alright, sweetheart. We’re so proud of you.” Daddy kisses my forehead.

Just seeing how happy this news made my parents makes me want to do even more to make them proud. They work so hard, so they deserve to have children who do the same.

Dear Lord, thank You so much for this opportunity to work for the STEM Society. I don’t know what I did to receive this incredible blessing, but I give all of the glory to You. I hope You know how happy this makes me, and I pray that working as a research assistant for them will prepare me for whatever You have in store for me in the future. In Jesus’ name I pray, amen.

After talking with my parents, I go back to my room and flop onto my bed. I really want to call Christian to share this news with him, but I don’t know if I should or not. Does he even want to talk to me right now? Is he mad at me because of the way that Truth treated his brother? Maybe I’ll just text him to see what happens.

I begin to type “Are you mad at me?”, but I don’t think that’s the best way to start this conversation. I don’t want to appear overly invested.

Love: Thank you for a great date, Christian.

Christian: I was just about to text you! Thanks for agreeing to go out with me. I loved spending time with you.

Love: I loved spending time with you, too!

Christian: Let’s do it again sometime ;)

I don’t know what to say to that. I really want to spend time with him again, but I don’t want to come onto him too strong too fast. This is all so new to me, and I don’t want to mess things up.

I’m so caught up in my thoughts that I barely notice my phone ringing.

“Hello?” I answer.

“Love, did I say something wrong? You didn’t respond to my text,” Christian says on the other end of the phone. I can’t believe he actually called.

“Oh no! You didn’t say anything wrong.”

“Are you sure?” he asks. “You must not want to hang out with me again.”

I laugh. “It’s not that. I was just thinking.”

“Thinking about what? Me and you?”

“Possibly.”

“Well?”

"Is Nehemiah still upset with Truth?" I ask, changing the subject.

"He calmed down a little bit, but he's still mad."

"Are you mad at me?"

I hope he doesn't see my sister's actions as a reflection of me. We're twins and all, but I would hate to have him think we're totally the same. By now, he should know that's not the case anyways.

"Why would I be mad at you?" Christian asks. "Our time together was perfect in my eyes."

"So, you really want to go out together again?" I ask.

"Yes! You thought I was playing?"

"I don't know," I respond. Why am I having such a hard time accepting the fact that he may be genuinely interested in me?

"Well, I'm not playing. I'm serious about getting to know you, Love, and possibly building something with you in the future. I even prayed about it."

"And what do you feel like God is saying to you?" I question, surprised that he has been praying about me and him.

"He's telling me to tell you to stop playing games and give me a chance," Christian says.

"Ha funny!" I laugh. "I thought I already gave you a chance."

"And that's it?"

Suddenly, Micah walks into my room. "It's time for dinner. Come on down."

"Dinner?" I ask. "It's only 5 o'clock."

"Yeah, dinner. Mama cooked early today."

"Alright, I'm coming," I respond.

"Who are you talking to?" Micah raises his brow.

"It's Christian," I say.

"Oh ok. Just come on down when you're done then."

"Christian, I have to go," I tell him. "I'll text you after dinner sometime."

"Sounds good to me," he responds. "Enjoy it, and think about what I asked you and let me know what you wanna do. Ok?"

"Ok," I say before ending the call.

After dinner Micah, Truth, and I are sitting in the living room watching the latest episode of Preacher's Sons. I don't watch TV much, so I haven't been keeping up with the show like Micah and Truth. Micah has his eyes glued to the TV, while Truth has her eyes glued to her phone.

"Love, let's go finish our homework," Truth says.

"I finished all my homework a while ago," I respond, confused because Truth never wants to do homework together.

"Can you help me with mine then?" she asks. "Please."

"Please? Where is the real Truth?" Micah breaks into a fit of laughter. We both know that Truth isn't the politest person on the planet.

"Quit playing, Micah. I really need help," Truth responds, rising from her seat on the couch. "Come on, Love."

"Alright then," I say, rising from my own seat.

I wonder what Truth is up to. She has a suspicious look on her face, so I highly doubt this is actually about homework.

"Where do you want to go?" I ask her.

"Let's go to my room," Truth says, already halfway up the staircase.

As soon as we're in her room, I ask "What's really going on?"

"Rue is coming to get me, and you're coming with me," Truth blurts out.

"Oh no I'm not!" I respond. I don't know who she thinks I am, but I want no part in this.

"Girl, come on! You get mad when I don't let you know stuff, and now you're mad when I do decide to tell you."

"Yeah because you're trying to do something stupid, Truth."

"And why is it stupid? Because it's not Nehemiah?" Truth rolls her eyes.

"Rue already played you once, so why are you giving him another chance to do the same thing? Didn't you learn your lesson?"

“Maybe I did, maybe I didn’t. Let me make my own mistakes.”

“I’m not about to help you do something stupid,” I reply. I really don’t understand her rationale. Rue clearly has something going on with Ariana, so I don’t understand why Truth thinks she stands a chance at actually making something work between the two of them.

“That’s your problem now! You’re so judgmental, Love.” Truth looks upset. “I’ll just go by myself.”

Feeling bad, I say, “Nevermind, Truth. I’ll go with you.”

“Didn’t I just say I’m going by myself? You can leave now.” Truth dismisses me from her room.

~10~

Innocence Gone

"God's will is for you to be holy, so stay away from all sexual sin. Then each of you will control his body and live in holiness and honor"

1 Thessalonians 4:3 NLT

Mercy

Me and Love have been talking on the phone for about an hour about everything from Truth and Rue to our upcoming college visits. We usually don't get to talk on the phone this much because me and Joel would typically be on the phone together. Since he's not talking to me, I'm free to talk to her and the rest of my girls as long as I want.

"Can I talk to you for a minute?" Joy asks, interrupting my conversation with Love.

"Yeah," I reply. "Love, can I call you back later?"

"Yeah sure," Love says. "Is that Joy?"

"Yeah, it's her."

"Tell her I said hi!"

"Ok, I will. Talk to you later," I say before hanging up the phone.

Joy and I haven't talked much since Wednesday night. I'm still really upset with her because I wish she would've told me first about her being raped before she told everyone else. That's something I thought a sister would do.

"What is it, Joy?" I ask.

"I just wanted to talk to you about the other night?" Joy says.

"What about the other night? You mean the other night when I found out you've been keeping secrets from me?"

"Mercy, I didn't tell you for a reason," Joy says, taking a seat next to me on the couch.

"And what was the reason? I really wanna know."

"I didn't want you to feel differently about me. I couldn't tell you to avoid certain things if you knew I was out there doing the same things I was telling you not to do."

"Joy, you're my sister! I wouldn't have viewed you differently. I would've been there for you through all of that," I say as a tear creeps down my face. "I can't believe you didn't think I would've wanted to know."

"Mercy, I was ashamed. I didn't want to tell anyone, not just you."

"But you just told everyone. I wish you would've told me before you told it to a room full of people. You owe me that respect."

"Please, don't make this all about you," Joy says. "You don't know what it feels like to be raped. You don't know the pain that I was going through. If you did, you would see why I wouldn't want to tell anyone, even you."

"So, what made you decide to tell everyone the other day?"

"I was tired of keeping it a secret. Holding on to past hurt hinders God from doing all He can in your life now."

"So how do you feel now?"

"I feel good," Joy says. "I feel free."

"That's good. I'm proud of you, sis," I say, hugging her.

I don't care what anyone says. The bond between two sisters is one of the biggest blessings God can give. My sister and I have been through a lot together. Aside from my clique, I know Joy is the one person that I can come to for literally anything.

When I release Joy, I ask, "Did Micah already know?"

"I had to tell him a while ago."

"Why?"

"I told him a couple of months after we started courting. We were walking through the park and he got too close to me and I started freaking out. It wasn't the first time it had happened, and he noticed it wasn't the first time too. Then he asked me what was wrong, and I told him."

"How did he respond?" I ask.

"He started praying," Joy says. "After that, I knew he was someone I could trust."

Sometimes I wish Joel was more like Micah. They're best friends, so I don't understand why Joel never prays with me, around me, or for me. Joy and Micah have such a God-centered relationship, and I want that.

"That's a blessing, sis."

After a few moments of silence, Joy asks, "So, how are you and Joel doing? I heard about what happened."

"He won't even talk to me, and I just don't get it. I've texted him like a hundred times, and I'm so annoyed," I say.

"Have you thought about how he feels though?"

After taking a second to think, I say, "No, not really."

"Well, put yourself in his shoes and see how you'd feel if he did what you did to him," Joy says. "Don't be so selfish."

Joy is right about me being selfish. That's one of my biggest struggles. However, I didn't tell Joy that Joel tried to feel up my skirt when he was taking me home, but I didn't want her to go back and tell Micah. Plus, that might make her stop liking him, and I don't need anyone else in this house trying to convince me to break up with Joel.

"So, what time do you have to go to the school for ACT prep?" Joy asks. My parents forced me to take this ACT prep course on Sunday afternoons as a part of my punishment for storming out of the house a few days ago. Luckily, Jael is doing it too.

"At 3:30," I respond. "What time is it?"

"It's almost 3:30. You better get going."

"You know I'm always late."

"Unfortunately, I know." Joy shakes her head.

"Whatever." I playfully shove Joy before grabbing my books and heading out the door.

After the ACT prep session, I'm mentally drained. We did an entire practice exam, so we can track our progress over the next few weeks. I scored a 25, and Jael scored a 26. The highest score came from Zeke. I can't believe he scored a 32, especially when the highest score you can receive is a 36.

"What are you about to do now?" Jael asks as we sit outside waiting on her ride to come. Everyone else left about ten minutes ago.

"I'm about to head home," I reply. "I'll probably try coming up with some new cheers for us to do at Friday's game."

"That's dope!" Jael says. "So, how did you get to hang out at Young Rue's crib the other day? I wanted to ask you earlier, but I didn't want to bug you because I'm sure everybody else was asking you the same thing."

I haven't talked much about that night to anyone besides Love, Ryann, and Ava, and I don't feel like talking about it right now. Messing around with Jesse was fun in the moment, but now I just want Joel. Cheering at the game Friday night made me miss my man. Every time the announcer called his name, I cheered as loud as I could. Unfortunately, I didn't feel the usual joy that I experience from cheering for him because I knew things weren't going well between us.

It has been four days, and Joel hasn't even attempted to make contact with me. I haven't received any calls, texts, or anything, and I don't even see him when we're at school. It's obvious that he's avoiding me.

"Truth is friends with Rue, and he invited us over. That's all," I say, keeping it short and sweet.

"How did they get to be friends?" Jael asks.

"I don't know," I lie. "You'll have to ask her that."

"Why didn't y'all invite me? I need me a rich and famous boo just in case medical school doesn't work out," Jael says.

"It was a last-minute decision," I respond. "Maybe next time though."

There won't be a next time anytime soon. I'm so mad at myself for getting so drunk around those guys. I bet they think I'm just another immature groupie, but I have to forgive myself for the way I acted. I'll just take it as a learning experience and never let it happen again.

"I can't believe Joel let you go over there though," Jael says.

"Joel doesn't tell me what to do." I roll my eyes. "I do what I want."

"Amen, sister!" Jael high-fives me. "I hate seeing girls let these dudes control them like they're married or something. Like, be independent. Have a mind of your own."

"Whatever you say!" I laugh. "I can't wait to see how you act when you finally get a man of your own."

"Nope," Jael says. "I'm not trying to get distracted by these dudes around here. My main focus is trying to get out of the hood, not getting stuck here."

"Boyfriends are fun though," I reply.

"Boyfriends are headaches too," she replies.

"They're that too," I agree.

"I bet," Jael says. "I need to tell you something though."

"What is it?" I ask.

"Did you hear about what happened at the party the other night?"

"No, what happened?" I decided not to attend the party this weekend because I knew Joel and I wouldn't be making an appearance together and none of my girls were going.

"Joel and Mercury left the party together."

"Huh? My Joel?" I don't believe I heard Jael correctly. Joel shouldn't have been at that party without me and especially not with his ex.

"Yeah, your Joel. You might want to ask him about that," Jael says. "My ride is here, so I'll catch up with you later."

"Alright, I'll talk to you later." I hug her before continuing to head to my car.

When I make it to my car that's parked near Panther Stadium, I notice Joel leaving the field. I wonder what he is doing here on a Sunday. He wasn't even at church this morning.

"Joel!" I scream to get his attention.

He keeps walking as if he doesn't hear me. We really need to talk, especially if what Jael just said about him and Mercury is true.

"Joel, I know you hear me talking to you!"

"Mercy, I don't wanna hear it," Joel replies. "I have somewhere to be."

"Exactly where do you have to be?" I rush toward his car door to block him from getting in. He's going to say something to me before he drives off this parking lot.

"None of your business, girl. Now, move."

"Make me." I cross my arms across my chest.

"You know I can. Why are you playing?"

"I'm not playing. You need to talk to me."

"We don't have nothing to talk about!" Joel says. "You made yourself look like the fool that you really are the other night, and I can't forgive you for that."

"You don't mean that," I say, tears welling up in my eyes.

"Yeah, I do mean it. I swear I mean it, Mercy."

My tears are now rapidly falling.

"What are you crying for?" Joel asks angrily. "You're the one who cheated."

"But Joel—"

"But Joel nothing," he cuts me off. "It's over. Give me my ring back."

After everything I've been through just to make this relationship work, I'm not giving up this easily. Joel is being so irrational right now, but if only he would listen to me, then maybe he would understand why I did what I did.

"Joel, let me explain!"

"You have nothing to explain to me. Get out of the way."

"Not until you listen to me."

"Why? You're not going to do nothing but lie to me. You're just like all of these other girls around here."

I throw my hands up in frustration. "What is that supposed to mean?"

"You see someone with some money and popularity, and you jump on them," he replies. "That's the only reason you're with me. You want to make yourself look good. You thought messing with that dude was going to give you some fame, but you just showed the world how dumb and fake you are."

"Wow," I respond. "If that's really what you think of me, then maybe we shouldn't be together."

As I try to get around Joel to head to my car, he pushes me against his car.

"I'm sorry," Joel says as he squeezes my arms.

"What are you doing?" I ask, wiping my tears with the back of my hands.

"Mercy, you slept with some dude that you barely even know the other night, but you won't even give me any play."

"I didn't sleep with anyone," I correct him. Because everyone saw me on Dame's Snapchat with him and the other guys, rumors have been spreading that I was sleeping around with at least one of them.

Inching closer to me, Joel whispers in my ear, "Get in the car."

"For what?"

"Because I said so."

Without further hesitation, I open Joel's driver's side door and crawl over to the passenger's seat. He rushes in behind me, slams the door, and speeds off.

"Wait, where are we going?" I ask.

"We're going to my crib."

"What for?"

"You'll see when we get there."

"Joel, I want to go home," I respond. I'm already in a lot of trouble for the way I ran off the other night, and I'm not trying to get into any more trouble. I was supposed to go to ACT prep and back home.

The five-minute drive that it usually takes to get to Joel's house from our school seemed like it was an hour long. I should be asking him what went down after the party last night with him and Mercury, but now doesn't seem to be the best time.

As soon as we pull into his garage, Joel rushes out of the car and hurries toward his front door without even attempting to open the car door for me.

"Come on!" Joel says.

"Joel, what are you doing?" I ask, slowly opening the car door. "Aren't your parents coming home soon?"

"Nope, they're on a business retreat, so this place is all ours."

"Joel, I don't—"

"Mercy, hush. Let's just get things between us back to the way that they're supposed to be."

"Ok." Going against my better judgement, I shut my mouth and follow Joel inside his house.

As soon as he shuts the door behind us, Joel begins to roughly kiss on me as he simultaneously leads me to his bedroom. My mind is screaming no, but my body is screaming yes. I know this is wrong.

I've been inside of Joel's house a few times, but I've never made it all the way to his room. I usually steer clear of his room because I know we might end up doing things we shouldn't be doing if we go in there. However, this time something is different. I feel like I owe this to him because of how badly I screwed things up earlier this week.

Once we're in Joel's bedroom, he picks me up and throws me on top of his massive bed. Then, he climbs on top of me.

"Joel, we shouldn't be doing this," I attempt to discourage him.

"Mercy, are you trying to make things right with me or not?" Joel momentarily stops.

After I don't say anything, he raises his voice, "Yes or no?"

I nod my head. Although I want to make things right with him, I know this isn't what I want to do. This isn't right.

"Don't say another word then," Joel says before yanking my skirt down. "I promise it won't hurt, Mercury."

Lord, please forgive me for what I'm about to do.

Ignoring the fact that Joel just called me by his ex's name, I internally pray as I cry silent tears and let my innocence slip away from me.

~11~

Trust Issues

"Trust in the Lord with all your heart; do not depend on your own understanding"
Proverbs 3:5 NLT

Truth

I probably shouldn't be meeting up with Rue, but I'm doing it anyways. I need to get some closure between us. Seeing him with Ariana left me so confused, and I'm curious to see what he has to say for himself. Love thinks this is a stupid idea, but I know this is something I need to do for myself.

Rue: I'll be there in two mins

Truth: K.

I wanted to meet up with Rue Saturday night, but I decided to wait until Sunday. I told him to meet me at the small coffee shop at the end of our block after I got home from church. The coffee shop isn't too far from our house, so walking wasn't a hassle. Plus, I wouldn't have to lie to my folk about where I was going. They know I'm going to the coffee shop, but they don't know I'm meeting Rue here.

Hearing my phone ring, I answer, "Hello?"

"I'm outside now," Rue says.

"Ok. You can come in," I respond.

"Come in?"

"Yeah, come in. What kind of question is that?"

Rue sighs. "You know I can't come in."

"Why not?" I ask, confused.

"If I'm seen with you, it'll be all over social media tomorrow."

"I don't care. Get in here, or I'm leaving." I hang up the phone. I don't have time for his nonsense.

A few minutes later, I notice him walking into the coffee shop. Once he steps into the door, he looks around to scope out the scene. Aside from me, there are about four other people in here, including the workers.

Walking to the booth where I'm sitting, Rue says, "What's up, Truth?"

"You tell me," I say, getting straight to the point.

"Are you mad?" he asks.

"What do you think? You made me look like a fool."

"I know."

"You know?" I raise my voice. "And you think that was ok?" I feel my blood pressure beginning to rise.

“Yeah, I know, but you have to understand that that wasn’t my intention. I didn’t want to hurt anybody’s feelings.”

“And you didn’t think being all lovey dovey with another chick in my face would hurt my feelings?” I yell.

“Can you lower your voice?” Rue asks. “I don’t want to draw attention.”

“Because you’re scared Ariana will find out? Is that the reason?”

“I don’t care about that girl.”

“Well, you could’ve fooled me.”

I don’t believe a word coming out of his mouth right now. If he doesn’t start telling me what I need to hear soon, I’m seriously going to bounce.

“Can you let me explain myself, Truth?”

“Go ahead, but if I even feel for a second that you’re lying to me, I’m leaving.”

“Don’t.” Rue looks me directly in my eyes. “Me and Ariana go way back. We met two years ago in the club. I wasn’t the same dude back then.”

“How were you different?” I ask.

“I was trying to impress my homies, and everybody knew Ariana and how she messed around with NFL and NBA players, rappers, and all that. I figured that messing around with her would give me some street credit,” Rue admits. I’m not even surprised he got with Ariana for that reason. I figure that’s what all of her dudes do.

"Did it work?"

"Not really," he replies. "She wouldn't go public with me because I was young and I hadn't really made it into the spotlight yet. While I actually started catching feelings for her, she kept going back and forth between athletes and rappers."

"Why didn't you just cut her off?"

"Because I liked the girl. Maybe even loved her." This is the most open he has been with me since we met each other.

"Do you still love her?" I ask.

Suddenly, a small voice interrupts us saying, "Excuse me? Are you Young Rue?"

"Yeah, I am," Rue replies, looking around to see who else is here again. It's still relatively empty in here.

"I love your music! Can I have a picture with you?"

Before Rue can answer, a woman who I'm assuming is the little boy's mama comes and snaps a picture.

"Thanks!" The boy hugs Rue. "Can you sign my hat?"

Rue pulls a Sharpie out of his pocket and asks, "What's your name, lil man?"

"Nehemiah," the little boy responds.

I immediately feel my whole body become tense after hearing that name. I was just with Nehemiah yesterday, and now I'm here with Rue. What am I doing with my life? I hope I didn't mess over a good guy for a trifling dude.

"Truth?" Rue says, interrupting my thoughts.

"My bad. What did you say?" The little boy and his mother are gone now, and I didn't even notice.

"You ready to go?"

"We aren't finished talking," I respond. I know he doesn't think he's about to get off this easy. He still hasn't explained why he played me the way he did.

Rue sighs. "What you want me to say?"

"Answer my question."

"What question?"

"Do you still love her, Rue?"

"No."

"Don't lie to me!" I raise my voice again.

"I don't love her, Truth. If I loved her, would I be here with you?"

I shrug. "Probably. I don't know about you."

"Truth, I don't know who you think I am, but I'm not a bad guy. Things with me and Ariana are just complicated right now."

"Why didn't you tell me that before then? Before I started catching feelings for you!" I hate being vulnerable, but I can't help it right now. I'm so upset, and I can't stop the tears from flowing from my eyes.

"I'm sorry," Rue says. "I didn't mean to hurt you like that. I really didn't. Trust me."

"How can I trust you? I can't trust nobody," I say, wiping my tears.

"Believe me when I say this. I don't love or even like Ariana. When I started getting gigs and stuff, she started catching feelings. That's how I knew she didn't want me for me, but she wanted me for the fame."

"That still doesn't explain why you're still messing around with her and buying her cars and stuff," I respond.

"Who the hell said I bought her a car?" Rue asks.

"She said her man bought her the car, and she said you were her man."

"You should've asked her which man because I'm not even her man."

"It sure looked like you were the other day. Explain that." I fold my arms across my chest. "And why did you lie about the reason that we were at your house that night?"

"Ariana runs her mouth, and I don't need everybody in my business."

"Answer my other question, too. I'm tired of you beating around the bush, Rue."

"I might not love her now, but I did love her at one point. I don't want to hurt her."

"Boy, get out of here! What kind of mess is that? You really expect me to believe that?" I begin to rise from my seat.

"Truth, listen. Don't go."

"Tell the truth then!" I get in his face.

"I am!" Rue pulls me back into the booth, so now I'm sitting right next to him. "I'm trying to end things with Ariana for good, but I don't know how."

"You need to figure it out then because I'm not sticking around waiting on you like a fool. I don't trust you," I respond.

"If you don't trust me, then what's the point of me even explaining myself?"

That's a good question. I don't think I can trust him, no matter how much I really want to. The whole Ariana thing really threw a curveball at me, so I don't know what to believe. He could be telling the truth, but he also could be feeding me lies like he was feeding Ariana the other day.

"I'm leaving," I say before rushing out of the coffee shop.

"Truth, don't go!" Rue says, chasing behind me. "I want you."

"I don't trust you, Rue!" I continue walking.

"Stop and listen to me, baby."

"Baby? I'm not Ariana." I smack my lips.

"Stop!" Rue says, grabbing me and forcing me to stop and look at him. "I don't want you, Truth. I need you."

"Need me for what, dude?"

"I just need you," he says. "You're the only one who listens to me and actually cares. You like me for me, and that's it. I can't lose you this soon."

When I look into his eyes, the emotion that I see seems real. What if he's not lying to me? Maybe he could be telling me the truth about him and Ariana. I don't know whether to try to trust him or keep it moving.

Suddenly, Rue's phone starts ringing, but he hesitates before answering it. When he picks it up, I clearly hear the voice on the other end of the phone.

"Tell Ariana I said she can have you," I say before walking away for good. Rue just stands there looking stunned and doesn't even try to stop me.

~12~

Talk to Me

"Be careful then, dear brothers and sisters. Make sure that your own hearts are not evil and unbelieving, turning you away from the living God."

Hebrews 3:12 NLT

Love

Dear Lord, thank You for an amazing church service today. After such a great week, it felt great being about to come into Your house and worship you. You've blessed me so much, and I'm so overwhelmed by it all. Thank You for allowing me to have a productive first week of classes. Thank You for blessing me with the internship with the STEM Society. I start next week, and I pray that You continuously strengthen me to do the work that You have called me to do. Open my mind to whatever it is that You want me to learn while being there. Also, thank You for blessing me with a blossoming relationship with Christian. I never expected this to happen because he's literally so perfect, God. It almost feels too good to be true. Please don't let it be. In Jesus' name, amen.

After church, Ryann and Ava agreed to come over like they usually do on Sunday afternoons. Mercy can't make it today because she's at ACT prep. I should probably be there too, but I prefer studying on my own.

"How was church today?" I ask Ava. Ava goes to a catholic church nearby, but sometimes her parents let her come to our church.

"Boring," she responds. "And some lady came up to me today and said something about the skirt I'm wearing."

"What about it?" Ryann asks as we both glance at the plaid skirt Ava has on.

"She said it was too short for church. I wanted to tell her to mind her business, but I know my parents would have had a heart attack." Ava rolls her neck. She's so feisty, but we all love it.

"It looks good to me," I respond.

"That's the problem with these church folks today. They're so judgmental," Ryann says.

"Not all church folks," I say.

"True," Ava agrees. "Why you hate church so much anyway?"

"Because of the way the last church I went to treated my family. They acted like we didn't belong there."

"How is that?" I ask.

"Y'all know Romeo has his whole left armed tatted up, right?"

"Yeah," Ava answers.

"I didn't know," I respond. I see Reagan at school a lot, but I usually don't bump into Romeo at all.

"Well, yeah he has all those tattoos. We were at church and this old lady came up to him and said the he might want to cover the tattoos up."

"What did he say to her?" I ask.

"He just laughed and walked away. He told me he couldn't believe that's how they greeted new guests."

"Yeah, that's kinda rude," I respond.

"Then, another lady came up to my mom and asked her where was her husband. When she told her she wasn't married, the lady asked her why she wasn't married."

"Are you serious?" Ava looks like she wants to go find the lady and fight her.

"Yeah, I'm serious." Ryann shakes her head. "I was really done with them after that."

"Do your other family members ever go back?" I ask.

"No," Ryann says. "My mom goes to church if she's off on Sundays, which is hardly ever. She doesn't make us go, but Reagan and River usually tag along with her."

"Do you think you'd ever go back?" I respond.

Ryann shakes her head. "Never."

This puts me in a difficult place because Ryann is one of my best friends. My religious life is such a huge part of who I am, and it hurts that I'm not able to fully share that side of me with her. I never know how she's going to respond, and I definitely don't want to push her away. I've been praying that somehow she gets to know God, but it doesn't seem like God is answering my prayers.

"Where Truth?" Ava asks.

"She went to the coffee shop down the street about an hour and a half ago, but she should be back soon," I respond. I wonder if that's really where she went because she seemed distracted in church today and she doesn't even like coffee. Knowing her, she's probably up to something.

"How is she? I feel like we haven't talked in forever," Ryann says.

"She's the same old Truth." I shake my head and laugh.

"I feel like she's avoiding me because she doesn't want to talk to me about her, Rue, and my cousin." Ryann laughs too. "I swear we haven't been around each other much since then."

"She might be," Ava says. "Are you close?"

"Yeah, I thought me and Truth were close," Ryann says.

"No. You and Ariana," Ava responds.

"Kinda," Ryann answers. "She doesn't come around much, but she's usually there when I need her."

"Were you the one who called her when Mercy and Truth needed a ride to Rue's place?" I ask.

"Yeah."

"Did you know about her and Rue?" I respond, curious to know.

"Yeah, I did."

"Did she tell you?"

"Nah. She brought him to our family reunion a couple of months ago. That's how I found out."

"Were they serious then?" I ask.

"I couldn't tell. He kinda stayed to himself while she went around talking to everyone. Their chemistry was off. It was awkward."

"You tell Truth you know about them?" Ava asks.

"I would've told her if she brought Rue's name up, but she never said anything to me about him. That's her fault for being so secretive." Ryann shrugs.

Figuring it's time to change the subject, I ask, "Do y'all want to go swim for a little bit?"

"Yep. You know we love your pool," Ava answers.

"Yeah, let's do it," Ryann says. "I could use a good swim before I go to work."

"I have some swimsuits that y'all can borrow," I say.

"Good. You know my parents so strict, and they won't by me two pieces. They only get me one piece." Ava shakes her head.

"Well, I've got your back." I wink before heading to my room to grab the swimsuits, so my girls and I can get some much-needed relaxation before the school week begins tomorrow.

When Ryann and Ava leave, I decide to fix myself a salad for dinner. Since I read online about how bad meat is for us, I've been cutting back on it. I might try to completely eliminate it from my diet, but I'm going to take some baby steps toward that goal first.

After I'm done eating, I review my notes from class last week and spend some quiet time with God. I've been trying to read through the whole Bible, and I'm so close to being done. I only have about two or three more books left.

I'm in the middle of my quiet time when I hear a loud thud outside my door.

"Hello?" I call out, but no one answers. My parents are gone out on a dinner date, Micah is out with Joy, and Truth is supposed to be home already but she's not.

I sit my Bible and cup of green tea on my desk, so I can see what's going on. When I open my door, I see Truth sitting on the floor with her head in between her knees.

"What's wrong, Truth? Are you ok?" I rush by her side.

"No, I'm not ok."

"What's going on?" I ask, taking a seat on the floor beside her.

"My life is a mess right now. You just don't understand."

"Tell me what's wrong."

"Rue got me all messed up."

"What did he do this time?" I shake my head.

After raising her head, Truth gives me the 411 on her meeting with Rue. I can't believe he disrespected her again. It's clear that there's more to him and Ariana than Rue is telling Truth. She just needs to let him go.

"I was feeling so good before all this happened. I made my mind up that this year was gonna be a great year for me, but now I can't even think straight. I went to the park to catch up on my readings for class, and couldn't even focus because of this dude. I can't get him out of my head." Tears start forming in Truth's eyes.

I can probably count on one hand how many times I've seen Truth cry, so I know she must really be hurting right now. I want to tell her what Ryann said about Ariana and Rue, but I don't think this is the best time since she's already hurting.

"Have you prayed, Truth?" I rub her shoulder to comfort her.

"Prayer hasn't even crossed my mind," Truth admits, wiping her tears. "I haven't been praying at all lately, even before all this stuff started happening."

"But why not?"

"I haven't been feeling it." Truth shrugs. "No matter how much Daddy and Mama make us go to church, I still can't find myself wanting to get closer to God."

"What do you mean?" Hearing my sister talk like this has me concerned. She has never said anything like this before.

"I'm not saying I don't believe in God. It's just that I wanna make my own choices. I feel like other people have more control of what I can and cannot do than I do myself."

"Like who?" I ask.

"Mama and Daddy force us to go to church all the time, and I don't complain. But whenever I wanna go do something that I wanna do, it's a problem. That's why I loved sneaking around with Rue. I felt like I was finally in control of something."

"Is that why it hurts so badly finding out that Rue isn't who you thought he was?"

"I guess so."

"What do you think all of this is showing you?"

"Well, I guess it's showing me that I might think I'm ready to be in full control of my life, but I might not be as ready as I think I am."

"That might be right." I nod my head. "What do you think you're going to do now."

"First of all, I'm deleting Rue's number. He's not about to play me again." Truth pulls out her phone and scrolls to Rue's name. "Better yet, I'm gonna block him."

"That's the Truth I know." I laugh and clap my hands. Truth has always had high standards for the people she allows in her life, and she has never been afraid to cut anyone off if they weren't living up to those standards.

"I'm trying to be a better person, but people always show me why I can't trust them," Truth says, shaking her head.

"That's why you have to put your trust in God," I respond. "People will always fail you, but God never will."

"Thanks, Love. I think I needed to hear that."

"I've got your back. I'm glad you decided to talk to me about all of this," I say. "Do you want to pray?"

"Yeah, I'd like that." Truth responds.

"Are you sure?" I ask, surprised she actually said yeah.

"Yeah, I'm sure," she replies. "Even though I said I hate being forced to go to church, I can choose whether I want to pray with you or not. I like that."

"Good." I smile.

"Ask me that more often. Maybe that'll make me want to pray more," Truth says.

"Ok, I will. Now bow your head and close your eyes," I say. I'm so thankful God allowed me and my sister to share this moment together, and I hope we can have more of these moments.

~13~

Come with Me

"My sheep listen to my voice; I know them, and they follow me."

John 10:27 NLT

Truth

I'm feeling great this morning! Last night's prayer session with Love was much needed, and I'm feeling better than I've felt in a really long time. Plus, I made a 98 on my AP Physics quiz this morning, which was the highest grade received by anybody in the class. Peter was looking pretty salty about that too.

"What did you make?" I ask Ava.

"I made a 83," Ava says. "I know Dad will be happy."

"That's good girl!" I smile.

"Yeah, I know." Ava smiles and pats herself on the back. "I worked hard to get a good grade."

"Where are you headed to now?" I ask.

"To the dance studio. We have practice at 4."

"Ok, I'll see you later then."

"Ok. Bye boo." Ava hugs me before walking away.

When I make it to my locker, I grab the books I need to do my homework tonight and put away everything I don't need. I don't need to grab anything for practice today because Coach Goodwin is out of town, so we won't have practice again until Wednesday.

"Truth, I'm disappointed in you," Zeke says, walking up to my locker.

"For what?" I ask.

"You didn't tell me you were Young Rue's girl?"

"What the heck are you talking about?"

"Check your Facebook."

Aw man. What the heck is going on here? I log onto Facebook and notice that I have hundreds of new friend requests from people I don't even know.

"What is all of this for?" I ask, wondering where all of these friend requests came from.

"Check your tag requests." Zeke responds.

"Lord." I look at my tag requests and see the photo that the little boy's mother took of me, Rue, and her son yesterday along with some other off-guard pictures.

"You've got some explaining to do." Zeke laughs.

"I don't have to explain nothing to nobody." I slam my locker shut.

I hear some girls laughing behind me. When I turn around, I see it's Mercury and her two minions, Ashley and Makayla. Great.

"What's so funny?" I turn all the way around to face them.

"You're what's funny." Ashley says, making her friends laugh. "What all did you have to do to make Young Rue go out with you?"

"Wait, do we even want to know?" Makayla adds before laughing again.

"She's just like Mercy. Birds of a feather flock together." Ashley high-fives Makayla.

"Don't even play with me. Y'all know me!" I step closer to them before Zeke grabs my arm. "Don't make me wipe the floor with your ratchet behinds. I have time today."

"I wanna see you wipe the floor then!" Ashley throws her bag on the floor, and a few people standing in the hallway begin looking our way.

"Chill out y'all," Zeke says.

"Let's just go," Mercury finally speaks up. "We don't have time for mess."

"Y'all better listen to y'all friend," I say.

"Whatever, trick," Ashley responds before walking away with her friends.

"You better walk away," I respond while they're still in earshot. "Let me go, Zeke." He slowly releases his grip on me.

I don't know why these girls decided to start beef with me this morning. I'm usually not one to entertain other people's pettiness, but I have a lot of pressure built up from everything that has been going on. I haven't had to whoop a girl in a minute, so they better leave me alone before they unleash a beast.

"How many people know about this?" I ask Zeke.

"Know about what?" he asks.

"About me and Rue?"

"The whole school is talking, and it's all over social media."

"That figures." I sigh.

"What you gonna do?"

"I'm gonna do me. That's all I can do. If everyone already knows, then I have nothing to hide." I don't mind having people's attention, but the attention I'm about to have because of my association with Rue is not what I want right now. At first, I loved the thought of being known as Rue's girl, but since I'm not sure whether he's trying to play me or not I would've preferred to keep us a secret a little bit longer.

"What about your boy though?"

"Who?" I roll my eyes.

"Nehemiah."

"That's not my boy."

"So, you don't really care what he thinks?"

"Hell no. He can think whatever he wants to think. I'm not his girl and never will be," I say before beginning to head to the parking lot. I'm going to try to catch a ride with somebody, so I don't have to wait until Micah finishes practice to go home.

"Why didn't you tell me though?" Zeke asks, following behind me.

"Because I don't have to tell you or nobody else nothing. Is that fine with you?" I roll my eyes.

"Lose the attitude, Truth."

"Who's gonna make me lose it?" I pause in my tracks. Zeke doesn't say anything. "That's what I thought."

"Girl, you're something else." Zeke shakes his head and laughs.

"I don't care." I begin walking again.

"Fine, Miss Hudson," Zeke says. "By the way, I heard you're taking all advanced classes now. Is that true?"

"Who told you that? And yeah it's true. Mrs. Dee made me change my schedule."

"I thought AP World History was the only AP class you were taking."

"Well, you thought wrong."

"Good. I always knew you were smarter than you think you are." I'm not even going to lie. Hearing that made me feel good because I honestly don't feel like I'm smart enough half the time.

"Thanks, Zeke." I smile.

"You're welcome," Zeke replies. "I'm here for you, too, if you ever need help with your work."

"I'll be sure to keep that in mind," I say, laughing.

"On a serious note, I know I wasn't the greatest boyfriend to you, but I'm gonna try to be the best best friend you've ever had."

"Really?"

"Yeah, I promise." Zeke looks over at me and smiles.

When we exit the front of the school, we see a huge crowd of people just standing there. It's not usually like this because people usually want to get off campus as fast as they can after being here all day.

"What's going on?" I ask Zeke. "Can you see?" I'm only 5'2, and Zeke is nearly 6 feet tall, so I know he can see over this crowd.

"Your boy is here?"

"Who is my boy?"

"Rue."

"Quit playing!" I shove Zeke.

"I'm not playing," he says. "See for yourself."

I begin to push my way through the crowd of people to see for myself. When I make it to the front of the crowd, Rue is in fact standing there beside his black Aston Martin coupe.

As soon as Rue spots me he says, "Come with me."

I stand there looking at him in disbelief. People have their phones out recording and taking pictures, and I don't know what to do. How dare he show up here like this after the way he played me again yesterday? He's the last person I expected to see standing out here.

~14~

Betrayed

"While they were eating, he said, "I tell you the truth, one of you will betray me."
Matthew 26:21 NLT

Mercy
Two days have passed. Two days have passed since I gave Joel what was meant for my future husband. Two days have passed, and I still don't know how I feel about all of this.

Ever since what happened with Joel, I feel like my relationship with God is in a terrible place. I have no desire to pray because I feel like God is so disappointed in me because I knew what I should have been doing but decided to go against what I knew God was telling me to do. I wish I could vent to my girls, but I'm too ashamed. All I can feel now is guilt and regret. My life is slowly falling apart.

When I finally look up from my desk, Ms. Hernandez is staring at me. I know I really haven't been paying attention in class these last couple of days, but hopefully she hasn't notice. She doesn't seem like the type to go back and tell my mom anyways, so I don't really care.

"Mercy, can I see you after class?" Ms. Hernandez asks.

"Sure," I respond. I really want to say no because I don't feel like talking to anyone right now, especially not some teacher.

"Class, your first exam will be this Friday," Ms. Hernandez proceeds to talk to the rest of the class."

"What is the exam on?" Zeke asks.

"It'll cover chapters 1 and 2 from last week," Ms. Hernandez responds. "Any more questions?"

"Will it be graded?" Zeke asks another question.

"No, I just like giving y'all tests for no reason," Ms. Hernandez answers with sarcasm. "Of course, it's going to be graded, Zeke." The whole room bursts out in laughter. Zeke is such a class clown, but he's probably the smartest one in the room. He's a lot smarter than what he lets other people think.

"I see you've got jokes," Zeke replies.

"I have a few in me." Ms. Hernandez smiles.

Right on time, the bell rings. As the rest of the class files out of the classroom, I slowly pack away my things.

"Come to my desk, Mercy. I have something to show you," Ms. Hernandez says after everyone has left the room.

"What is it?" I ask.

"It's a letter for you. Come look."

"A letter from who?"

"Here," she says, handing me a large, white and gold envelope.

"Why is it already opened? You're just like my mom when she says I have mail."

"I was curious. Sorry." Ms. Hernandez laughs.

The envelope is from the Georgia State Senate. When I open the envelope, I'm surprised to see this invitation to attend this Youth Summit at the Georgia State Capitol next month.

"Wow. This is amazing," I say. "How did I get this?"

"This is the first time our school has been selected to send a representative to this summit, and I recommended you because I knew you'd represent our school well."

This is strange. Ms. Hernandez doesn't even know me. I've only been in her class for a week and a half. Before then, we had had only one interaction and that was when she was sitting in on a student council meeting.

"You're a natural leader, Mercy. I noticed that even before you were in my class. If you stay focused, you have the ability to do great things in our community and beyond."

"Thanks," I reply, not knowing what else to say. This is the first good thing that has happened to me since last week.

"You're welcome," Ms. Hernandez responds. "Are you alright though? You haven't been yourself in class lately, and I'm concerned."

"I'm good," I lie. "I've just been busy lately."

"I just hope you're busy with the right things, Mercy. You have a bright future ahead of you, and I would hate to see you not reach your full potential."

"I understand," I respond. I don't feel like being lectured right now.

"Good. I'll see you tomorrow. Enjoy the rest of your day." Ms. Hernandez hugs me.

"Thank you," I reply, hugging her back before heading to my next class.

When it's time for cheer practice, I am glad because sometimes I feel like cheerleading is the only thing that is able to keep my mind off of things.

"What's up with you?" Truth asks, sitting beside me to begin stretching. "I feel like you've been avoiding us all week."

"Yeah, are you ok?" Love sits down on the other side of me.

"I'm totally fine." I fake smile.

"Well, why have you been M.I.A?" Truth responds.

"I've been busy with student council stuff," I lie. Love looks at me like she knows I'm lying, but doesn't say anything.

"I have a lot of stuff to tell you, girl," Truth says.

"About what?" I ask.

"About Rue." Truth shakes her head. I should've known this was where this conversation was going. Everyone saw him pick her up from school the other day, and those pictures that were posted online of them the other day have been circulating through all of the major blogs.

“What about him?”

“This dude tried to apologize to me with an expensive handbag when he picked me up the other day. He didn’t even have anything to say for himself.”

“What did you say to him?” I ask.

“I told him that he must think I’m Ariana or something. Then I told him to take me home, and he did.”

“Have you heard from him since then?” Love asks.

“His number is still blocked, so nope,” Truth responds.

“When did you block him?” I ask.

“See, that’s how you know you’ve been M.I.A. I haven’t even told you about how he tried to play me at the coffee shop the other day,” Truth says before bringing me up to date on everything that has happened between them since we last talked.

“Wow, that’s crazy.” I shake my head. I know me and Joel have our issues, but I’m glad he’s not out here disrespecting me like Rue is disrespecting Truth.

After we’re done stretching, Coach Goodwin blows her whistle and says, “Everybody get in your stunt groups! Makayla and Ashley, since Jael is out for this weekend, I’m going to need you girls to base Mercy by yourselves. You both are seniors, so I know you can handle it,” Coach Goodwin says.

"Yeah, we can do it," Ashley answers.

"We got this," Makayla says, flexing her little muscles.

"Alright, let me see Mercy in a liberty then," Coach Goodwin instructs.

I can't stand these girls, but I must admit they are pretty solid as bases.

"Five, six, seven, eight...," Coach Goodwin counts off.

Then, I am lifted into the air with such great strength, considering it's only two girls underneath me. When I'm at the top of the stunt with arms outstretched into a high V in the air, I smile because I am impressed with my bases.

"Excellent job! Now cradle!" Coach Goodwin yells from below. "Five, six, seven..."

Before Coach Goodwin can even make it to eight, Makayla and Ashley suddenly drop me from the stunt and onto the hard ground on my back.

"What the hell was that?!" Coach screams as I lie on the ground.

I feel like I can't even move, but from the corner of my eye I notice Truth and Love running over to me.

"Are you ok, Mercy?" Love asks, worriedly.

"If she's hurt, you broads are going to have to answer to me!" Truth threatens Makayla and Ashley. "I know y'all dropped her on purpose!"

"Now why would we do that, Truth?" Makayla asks with a sinister grin on her face. If I wasn't still on this ground, I would smack that grin right off of her face. I know they dropped me on purpose. There's no way that should have happened.

"Shut up!" Coach Goodwin says. "Mercy, do you think you can move?"

"Yeah, just give me a minute," I respond. I don't feel anything from the impact, but the shock of it all is what hurts.

"Makayla and Ashley, what happened?!" Coach asks, turning her anger back to the two hating chicks that dropped me.

"I don't know, Coach," Makayla says, pretending to be clueless.

"Mercy did something weird in the air before the cradle," Ashley says, falsely blaming me. "Mercury never did what Mercy just did, so we were just caught off guard. Sorry."

"They bring up Mercury a lot, so why isn't Mercury on the team anymore anyways?" Olivia attempts to whisper to Love. However, I'm sure the whole team heard that. She can't whisper at all.

"Well..." Makayla begins with another smirk on her face.

"Well, let's just say she has other priorities right now that are more important than being on this team," Ashley finishes for Makayla.

"What other priorities? I know she's not in anybody's church, and I know she isn't the smartest girl ever," Truth says, throwing major shade.

"Truth, chill," Love says, nudging Truth in the ribs.

"I'm just being honest!" Truth puts her hands in the air, feigning innocence.

"She might not be the smartest, but she sure isn't the dumbest," Makayla says, looking directly at me as I slowly make my way up from the ground.

What the heck is she just staring for? She should've been helping me up since she's part of the reason that I was on the ground in the first place.

"I believe I was talking to you, so direct your comments to me and not Mercy," Truth continues, not backing down. Love shakes her head because she knows how hard it is to stop Truth when you get her riled up.

"Maybe she's looking at Mercy because she is the dumbest," Ashley says.

"Excuse me?" I respond. How did I even get put in this? I know I'm not about to stand for any disrespect on my own team, especially after I was just dropped in front of everyone.

"You heard me, Mercy! You just might be the dumbest girl that we know," Ashley yells toward me.

"Ain't no might! She is the dumbest girl that we know. By the way, does your dumb self even know that Joel is about to be Mercury's baby's daddy?" Makayla asks, shocking everyone, including me.

This can't be true. These girls are lying. Mercury cannot possibly be pregnant, especially not by Joel. He's mine and everyone knows it, including her.

"Oops! Judging by the look on her face, I guess not," Ashley adds, holding back laughter as I'm holding back tears.

"I hope you didn't think Joel was being faithful to you," Makayla says. "He's been cheating on you the whole time you were out here flaunting like y'all have the most perfect relationship."

"He and Mercury have something real going on," Ashley says. "Something you wish you had."

This could explain why Joel was trying to brush off Mercury's remarks on the way to class on the first day of school. This could explain why he went days without seeing me this summer. This could explain why Mercury is as big as ever now. This could explain why she removed herself from the team before the start of her senior year, the most anticipated year of high school. This could explain why Joel went all out with his now meaningless promises, promise ring, and homecoming proposal. He knew he was doing me wrong behind my back, and he wanted to make up for it. That's the only explanation.

As if on cue, Joel looks my way from the end zone of the football field and waves at me. The only thing I can do is stare at him. I can't even muster up the strength and dignity to wave back to him, so I just look back at him with a face full of disgust. How could he do this to me? How could he do this to us? How could he just take my virginity knowing that he was doing me wrong all along?

Before I know it, the tears begin to overtake me, and I can't stop them from falling. At this point, I don't even care that I'm surrounded by all of my teammates, including the two hating cheerleaders responsible for literally ruining my life with the news that they just shared with me and everyone else on the team. I've never felt so betrayed.

"God, please don't let this be true," I pray before bolting off from the football stadium, leaving my team behind.

~15~

Real Friends

"There are 'friends' who destroy each other, but a real friend sticks closer than a brother."
Proverbs 18:24 NLT

Truth

I'm pissed. Coach Goodwin made us run a mile for arguing at practice after Mercy was dropped. It wasn't my fault that Makayla and Ashley were disrespecting Mercy for the millionth time. I feel like they should've been the ones getting punished instead of the whole team, but whatever though.

I'm worried about my girl Mercy though. I don't know if the rumors are true about Joel having a baby on the way with Mercury, but if they are, that's so messed up. For Mercy's sake, I hope they're not true.

As I see Micah walking toward his car, where Love and I are standing and waiting, I get even madder.

"Micah, you knew?! Why didn't you tell us, man? You had our girl out there lookin' like a fool!" I scream, holding nothing back.

"Love, what is she talking about?" Micah asks, ignoring me and looking at Love, the rational one, for a clue as to what is going on.

"Joel and Mercury! That's what I'm talking about. You knew?" I ask again, before Love has a chance to respond. I know I should calm down, but right now I just don't want to.

"Hold on, what?" Micah asks, looking dumbfounded.

"That's your best friend! Stop looking stupid. You know what I'm talking about," I respond, storming toward his side of the car.

"Truth, shut up." Micah puts his hand in my face to silence me. "Love, what's going on?"

"Is Joel still messing around with Mercury, Micah?" Love asks, sounding like she was the one who was cheated on.

Without saying anything, Micah marches off toward the football field. Without hesitation, Love and I follow him. I don't know what he is about to do, but I do know that when Micah is silent it is a scary thing. He's pissed right about now, and judging by the way he reacted, I'm starting to think that maybe he didn't know anything about this whole Joel and Mercury thing after all.

"Joel, come here, man!" Micah yells when he spots Joel on the sidelines talking to another football player.

As Joel begins to jog his way over, I feel my blood begin to boil. Unfortunately, as I prepare to charge at him, Love grabs my arm.

"Don't even think about it, Truth," she says. I think I'm going to listen to Love this time though. I feel like Micah is going to handle this situation a lot better than I ever could.

"What's up, man?" Joel asks.

"What's this I hear about you and Mercury still messing around?" Micah asks, wasting no time.

"Man..." Joel sighs, putting his head in his hands. "Who told you that?"

"Does it matter who told him? All that matters is that our girl ran off at practice crying because of some mess she heard about you and Mercury! Are you about to be a daddy?" I shout. I don't know why he's looking so embarrassed. What you do in the dark is always bound to come to the light.

"Man, tell me this isn't true. Please, tell me you didn't go and get that girl pregnant," Micah pleads, looking like he's on the verge of tears himself. I know that Joel is his boy and all, so it must hurt even more that he had to hear something life-changing like this from his little sisters.

"Bro, I don't know," Joel says.

"What you mean you don't know?" I say, charging at Joel once again. This time Love isn't quick enough to grab me, and I'm right in his face. I'm not going to hit him yet, but I do want some answers.

"I messed up," Joel says, stepping away from me. I move right along with him. If he says one more thing I don't like, I'm going to hit him right in his mouth. I don't believe him fooling around with Mercury was a mistake. He knew what he was doing, and I have no sympathy towards him.

"So, it's true?" Micah asks. I know he's disappointed that the one guy who he treated like a brother would betray him and the girl that he calls his sister like this.

"I don't know if it's true or not," Joel responds.

"Did you sleep with her?" Micah asks, rage noticeably forming in his eyes. If looks could kill, Joel would be one dead jock.

"Mercury or Mercy?" Joel asks.

"Boy, I will take you out right now! Don't play with me like that. You know me!" Micah yells as he points his finger in Joel's face and steps up to him.

"Truth, move," he says to me. I listen because I don't want to be in the way if this does come to blows.

"Come on, Micah. This dog isn't even worth it. Let's go," Love says, grabbing Micah's arm.

"You girls can go back to the car," Micah replies, not looking away from Joel's face. "I want to see what this dude has to say for himself."

"You know me, man. You know I'm not perfect," Joel says, trying to plead his sorry case.

"I never said you were perfect, man! The problem is that you can't respect yourself enough, or Mercy for that matter, to keep that thing in your pants," Micah responds.

That's the sad thing about guys. They pride themselves on sleeping with as many girls as they can whenever they can. The sad part is that they don't even realize the negative effects of their actions. Once a girl is cheated on, her whole mindset is messed up. She starts thinking that she was the one in the wrong, but most of the time it doesn't even have anything to do with her.

"Mercy wasn't putting out at the time, and Mercury was. I didn't mean to hurt her, but I have needs, too!" Joel says.

"You sound so foolish right now, Joel," I say. I expected better from him, but clearly he's just another one of these dogs roaming around here.

"You know what, man? I'm glad you hurt Mercy," Micah says, nodding his head.

"Huh? Why?" Joel asks, just as confused as I am.

"I'm glad you hurt her, so she can see that she deserves better than you. Stay away from Mercy, and stay away from me too. We ain't cool. We ain't brothers. We ain't nothing no more, man," Micah says. "Let's get out of here, girls."

"Bro, wait," Joel says, reaching out to Micah.

"Man, did I stutter? You ain't nothing to me no more," Micah replies, visibly hurt. I have never seen my brother this angry and disappointed before, and I can't resist what I'm about to do next.

I draw my arm back as far as I can, and bless Joel's left eye with my right fist. I should've hit him in the mouth too. No one hurts my brother, my twin, or any of the other girls that I consider to be like sisters to me without suffering the consequences. Real friends stick up for each other no matter what.

When we make it back to Micah's car, he says, "I have ten missed calls from Joy."

"You think she already knows?" Love asks.

"As much as people gossip at that school, the whole school probably knows by now," I say.

"Dang, I'm gonna hate having to make this call back to her," Micah says.

"I'll call Mercy and check on her," Love says.

"No, give her some time," Micah says. "I'll call Joy, and I'll ask how she's doing then."

"Sounds good," Love responds.

"Do y'all wanna go get food before the scrimmage or will y'all get something from the concession stand?" Micah asks. I forgot we told Ryann we were coming to their scrimmage game today. I'm not even feeling it anymore, but that's my girl and I have to support her.

"Yeah, I guess," I answer.

"You guess what?" he asks.

"We can eat there," I respond.

"Either is fine with me," Love says.

"Ok cool," Micah says. "I'll call Joy, but y'all can go ahead to the game. I'll be there in a minute."

"Alright," Love says before walking away.

Love doesn't say anything on the short walk to the gym, and I don't say anything either. I didn't know high school could be this stressful. Last year was nothing compared to all of the drama we're experiencing this year, and this is only the second week of school.

When we make it to the gym, I immediately break out in a sweat. It's like 100 degrees in here. I don't know how the players do it. I'm thinking about heading back out the door, but I can't do Ryann like that. My edges are already sweated out from practice anyways.

Even though this is only a girls' scrimmage game, there are a lot of people here supporting them. Me and Love decide to sit close to the bottom so we can have a good view of Ryann. Shortly after, Micah walks in and joins us.

"Did you talk to Joy yet?" Love asks.

"Yeah," he replies.

"What did she say?" I ask.

"I promise I could tell she was so close to cursing me out. Thank God she didn't."

"She thinks you knew about Joel and Mercury, too?" I ask.

"Too?" Micah raises his brow at me.

"You know what I mean," I say. "You know I assumed you already knew about it."

"Oh yeah I know that," he says. "But yeah, she thought I knew too."

"So, are you two still good?" Love asks.

"Of course. That's my baby." He smiles. He loves that girl so much, and I'm so jealous.

"Good," Love and I say together.

"She said Mercy was taking everything hard," Micah reveals.

"What was she doing when you called?" I ask.

"Burning up stuff," Micah says.

"Burning up what?" Love asks.

"Apparently she piled up all of Joel's stuff and set it on fire."

"Dang, our girl is a savage!" I laugh, slightly amused.

Suddenly one of Young Rue's songs begins blasting through the speakers, and our girls' basketball team runs onto the court.

Love nudges me and says, "There goes your boy."

"Whatever," I say, searching for Ryann on the court. "How do you even know this song?"

"I looked up some of his music the night after you first told me about him," Love responds.

"Oh."

I'm not about to worry about Rue right now. I need to get myself together before I try to take on him and the mess that comes with him. I'm young, so I have plenty of time to worry about a boyfriend. Plus, I've been kinda stuck on what Nehemiah said to me the other day. He's right. I deserve so much more than what I'm allowing myself to put up with.

"There's Ryann," Micah says, pointing at our girl. She's still rocking number 9 like her favorite NBA player, Tony Parker, from the San Antonio Spurs.

"Let's get it, Ryann!" I stand to my feet to cheer her on.

"Go Lady Panthers!" Love stands and chants.

Shortly after, the game is underway. Within minutes, our girls are up 12-2 against Atlanta Tech. Ten of those twelve points were scored by Ryann.

"Ryann has been grinding in the gym," Micah says. "It's paying off."

"That's what you call dedication," Love says.

By halftime the score is 42-22. Ryann has scored 25 points already.

"Look at Ava!" Love yells as the KHS Step Team takes the floor. Ava has the most rhythm that I've ever seen, and I'm not only speaking amongst Asians. I don't know where she got it from, but she's the best one on our step team.

"I see you, Ava!" I scream to hype her up.

When "Freedom" by Beyoncé starts playing, the girls start to do their thing. With all their stomping and jumping around, clapping, and hair slinging, they look good. They never fail to impress.

Once their routine is over, everyone stands to clap and the basketball teams run back onto the floor.

"Hey, we didn't see y'all walk in," Christian says, walking up the steps to the row where we're sitting. Nehemiah is right behind him. Suddenly, I feel butterflies, but I don't even know why.

"What's up, y'all?" Nehemiah greets Micah with a handshake and Love with a hug before pausing in front of me.

"Are you just gonna stand there?" I ask with a little attitude.

"Well, hello to you too, Truth." He laughs before taking a seat next to me.

"Hey."

"Dang, what's wrong with you Truth?" Christian laughs.

"Nothing," I say. "I'm just tired."

"I feel you," Christian says. "How are you, Love?"

"I'm alright." Love blushes as Christian takes a seat on the other side of Micah.

"Ryann is really good, huh?" Nehemiah says.

"Yeah, she had an amazing season last year," Christian replies. "I can't wait to see what she does this year."

"What up?" Ava says, joining us as well.

"Hey girl!" Love greets her. "You girls were great out there."

"Thank you. We know." Ava flashes a big smile.

"Dang, cocky much?" I laugh.

"Never cocky. Always confident, boo," Ava responds, squeezing between me and Nehemiah.

"Ryann is balling!" Micah says. Looking up at the scoreboard, I see the score is now 65-30. Ryann has scored 12 more points.

With two minutes left on the clock, Ryann takes a shot from long range and misses. She goes up to get her own rebound, but before both of her feet are solidly planted onto the floor, she hits the floor and grabs her knee. Without hesitation, the six of us rush onto the floor.

"Ryann, are you ok?" Love asks.

"Back up! Back up!" Coach K, the girls' basketball coach, demands.

"We're not going anywhere while our friend is lying on the floor!" I yell back.

Tears are now rolling down Ryann's face as she continues to grope her knee.

"Please no!" Ryann yells between cries. "Let's pray!"

"Let's what?" Love asks. Ryann is an atheist, so this is shocking to all of us.

"Pray!" Ryann screams, her face writhing in pain.

"Ryann, the ambulance is on the way," Coach K says. "Do you think you can get up?"

"God, no!" Ryann continues to cry. "God, if you exist I'm sorry! I'm so sorry, God!"

"Ryann, you're going to be ok." Love tries to comfort her.

I don't know what to say. I've never seen our girl in this much pain, and I've never been the comforting type.

Help us, Lord.

Seemingly ignoring Love, Ryann goes on "Please don't let it be over for me, God! I promise I'll do right if I make it through this. Please, God! Save my career. I'm begging you! I need you. I want you, Lord. Forgive me for not calling on you until now."

"I think we should carry her to my car," Micah offers as Ryann continues to cry hysterically. "We'll make it there a lot faster if we do that instead of waiting on the ambulance."

"Good idea," Christian agrees. "You go get your car and bring it to the front. Nehemiah and I will carry her to the car."

"Thanks a lot guys," Coach K says as Micah sprints out the gym doors.

"Lord, please let her be ok," Nehemiah prays. "Truth, hold my phone and keys while we help her up."

I don't say anything. I take his phone and keys without hesitation.

"Thanks," Nehemiah says to me. "Bro, are you ready?"

"Yeah," Christian answers. "Ryann, we got you. Ok?"

"I don't think I can get up," Ryann says.

"You don't have to do anything, Ryann. We got you," Nehemiah says

"You got big, strong men. You be ok," Ava says.

Within a matter of seconds, the guys have Ryann lifted and her arms draped across their shoulders. The entire gym erupts in applause as we begin to exit.

"There he is," I say, spotting Micah parked right beyond the exit doors.

After carefully placing Ryann in Micah's car, Christian says, "We'll meet y'all at the hospital. The girls can ride with us."

"Alright, man." Micah speeds off.

"Truth, can you ride with me?" Nehemiah asks.

"Why can't I ride with Christian?"

"Look, Truth. Chill with the attitude because now is not the time for this. I need someone to direct me to the hospital, so will you ride with me or not?" Dang, his commander-like tone got me in check.

"Yes, sir," I sarcastically respond.

"I'll ride with Christian, and I'll try to reach Ryann's family on the way over," Love says.

"I ride with them, too," Ava says. Great. Now it's just me and Nehemiah.

Walking over to Nehemiah's car, he says, "Hand my keys over."

I hand them over and ask, "What about your phone? Don't you want it, too?"

"No, you can hold onto it for me," Nehemiah says, opening the door to his car for me. That's surprising. Most guys wouldn't let a girl keep their phone in a million years. They always act like they have something to hide when it comes to their phones. I click the home button to see if he has a passcode, and he doesn't.

Noticing what I just did, Nehemiah enters his car and says, "Unlike some guys, I have nothing to hide from you, Truth."

"What's that supposed to mean?" I roll my eyes.

"Why are you so in denial? You know you deserve more, and you know I can give it to you," Nehemiah says, beginning to drive away from the parking lot. "But you keep expecting to get love from a dude like Young Rue who never could love you the way you need to be loved."

"How do I know what you can give me? I barely even know you."

"But you know I'd never hurt you. You can't tell me that you don't feel that."

"Feel what?"

"My sincerity."

"I don't trust you or anybody else."

"Why? Because some dude broke your heart?" Nehemiah asks. "I'm not him."

"Nehemiah, we won't work!" I yell with tears forming in my eyes.

"Why, Truth?" He hits the brakes on the car. "Just tell me why."

"I'm a mess! If you think you want somebody like me, you must be messed up too. Don't you get it?"

"No," he raises his voice. "I don't get it at all."

I throw my hands up in frustration. "Can we not do this now?"

"You're right." He gets the car moving again. "But we're revisiting this conversation and that's that."

~16~

Hurt Bae

"Feel my pain and see my trouble. Forgive all my sins."
Psalms 25:18 NLT

Mercy

I've been sitting in our backyard for the past four or five hours wondering why God is punishing me like this. I know I've been doing a lot of sinning lately, so I guess it's true when they say you reap what you sow.

"God, I just don't understand right now. I thought Joel and I were planning on spending the rest of our lives together. He betrayed me, Lord, and yet I still can't think of anything I want more than to be with him. How can I forgive him and move on from this? Lord, please help me. I know I can't do this on my own. Was I not enough for him? Or was I just too much for him? God, I'm hurting! Please, give me the strength to make it through this." I cry out as I fall to my knees next to the ashes that remain from all of Joel's things that I burned up.

"Mercy, are you ready to talk now?" Joy walks out the door to the backyard.

"No! I just need to be alone," I reply.

"You can't do this all night," Joy says, sitting next to me on the grass.

"What else can I do? My life is ruined, and I'm so embarrassed."

"All you can do is move forward, sis."

"But how? Joel made me feel bad for fooling around with Jesse, and I slept with him because I wanted him to forgive me. Then, he made me look stupid in front of my whole squad by getting Mercury pregnant."

"You slept with him, Mercy? I thought you were waiting." Joy's eyes begin to water.

"I told him I didn't want to, but I figured it was the only way I could make things right between us," I admit.

"I'm so sorry," Joy says. "I can't believe he did this to you."

"I'm sorry too." I lean my head on Joy's shoulders and weep.

After I cry on Joy's shoulders for about twenty minutes, Joy says, "I want you to know that God forgives you."

"Are you sure?" I look up at Joy.

"Yes, I'm sure," she responds. "God says it countless times in the Bible that He forgives us when we sin, no matter how bad we feel the sin is. That's something I wish I had told myself when I was feeling ashamed of my past sin."

"How did you get over the hurt from your past?" I ask.

"You have to keep reminding yourself of what God says about you in His Word. You're beautiful and loved by Him no matter what, and He has a purpose for everything He does in your life."

"What do you think the purpose is for everything that just happened with Joel?"

"Honestly, Mercy, I don't know. Maybe all of this happened to show you that Joel isn't the guy for you."

"Did God really have to hurt me just to show me that?"

"Sometimes He hurts you in order to pull you closer to Him."

"I never really thought about it that way," I respond. "But ever since I slept with Joel, I haven't been praying or anything. That hurt me, so why didn't that pull me closer to God?"

"I don't know. Sometimes God pulls on us, but we're too busy running away from Him that we don't even notice. Does that make sense?"

I nod. "Yeah, I can relate to that."

"Just don't keep running from Him. Ok?"

"I won't."

When I finally decide to come in the house, I turn my cell phone off. I have a lot of missed calls and texts from my girls and my punk ex-boyfriend, but I need to spend some time alone now. Whenever I'm feeling emotionally drained, I usually try to sleep it off. Unfortunately, this pain I'm feeling now is something I've never experienced before. It is the pain of my first heartbreak.

My mother made rice, chicken, and arepa for dinner tonight. Arepa is one of my favorite Dominican desserts, but I don't even have the strength to stomach food right now. I guess I'll just hang out in my room.

I feel this strong urge to read my Bible because it might take my mind off of things, so I begin by doing a word search on my Bible app. As I type "pain" in the search bar, a lot of scriptures pop up. Where do I even begin?

The first scripture I click on doesn't seem to be relevant to what I'm feeling, so I move on to the next one. This one is even less relevant to me than the first one, so I exit the Bible app and click on Facebook. The first thing I see is a picture of Mercury holding her bulging stomach. The caption reads, "Thank God for blessing me and Joel Jackson with a healthy bundle of joy." The picture has 250 likes, 102 comments, and 53 shares. Are you freaking serious?

Since I'm already here, I decide to go ahead and read through the comments. Most of them are some form of

"Congratulations" and "You're going to be a great mom." Lies. How is she going to be a great mother with someone else's man? How can they even congratulate her for getting pregnant out of wedlock with someone else's man?

Scrolling further through the comments, I see someone asked her when is the baby's due date. Mercury replied, "On Valentine's Day/February 14th <3". Great. That means this baby was conceived around June, and that Mercury is already two months pregnant. I seriously can't believe Joel was messing around on me all this time, and I was oblivious to the whole thing.

"God, what did I do to deserve this?!" I scream as I hurl my phone across the room.

Abruptly, someone begins knocking at my door, asking, "Can I come in?" It's my mother.

"Sure," I respond. "You can let yourself in."

"What's the matter, baby?" she asks, coming over to caress my hair like she used to do when I was upset when I was a little girl.

"Me and Joel broke up," I say.

"Are you ok? What happened, sweetie?"

"No, I'm not ok. He cheated on me and got a girl pregnant. How am I supposed to be ok after that, Mom?" I roll my eyes.

"Mercury Myles?"

"Bingo."

"Have you two talked about it?" Mom asks.

"No, we haven't talked about it. What more is there to say? I don't ever want to see or talk to him again."

"If you two haven't talked about it, then you haven't really broken up. Have you?"

"I guess you're right," I admit. "But how am I supposed to be able to talk to him after finding all of this out?"

"Mercy, you're a strong, smart girl. You can do this. I know you can," Mom says, rubbing my shoulders.

"But I'm not ready yet," I respond.

"Take however much time you need, baby. Cry if you need to, but remember this pain won't last forever." I don't know why, but when my mom says this I'm instantly reminded of the story of Job in the Bible. He literally lost everything he had, including his loved ones, but God eventually blessed him two-fold because He knew the type of man that Job was. I can find comfort in this story alone.

"Thanks a lot, Mom." I hug her before she gets up to exit my room.

I'm really glad she didn't point out that her and Daddy have been right about Joel all along, even though I clearly didn't see it. I was so convinced that Joel was the perfect guy for me that I didn't even stop to think for a second that he could possibly be something totally different than I imagined.

I don't really know how I'm supposed to move forward, but I know it's something I must do. For the past year, I've been so consumed with Joel and Mercy and Mercy and Joel that I've forgotten what it means to focus solely on me.

As I walk over to sit in front of the mirror of my vanity, I realize I don't seem to recognize the face staring back at me. This is the face of shame, hurt, guilt, and regret. I know I caused some of this, but a great deal of it was out of my hands. Who would've known sophomore year of high school would knock me off of my high horse this quickly?

I have pictures from freshman year and junior high school posted along the outline of my mirror. Staring at these photos reminds me of the girl I once was. I used to be so focused on school, cheerleading, church, and whatever else I thought was good for me. It's time for me to get back to the old Mercy. I lost myself in my relationship with Joel, but that's over with. I've cried enough, and I refuse to cry anymore.

"Lord, bless the man who dared to break my heart," I pray as I grab the scissors from the top drawer and chop off my butt-length, luscious locks. Then, I pick up my phone to text Joel.

Mercy: It's over.

~17~

Forever Loyal

"Many will say they are loyal friends, but who can find one who is truly reliable?"
Proverbs 20:7 NLT

Love

I don't know when, but somehow I drifted off to sleep right on the couch in the waiting room. I glance at the clock, and it's 11:32 pm. We're still at the hospital with Ryann waiting on the results of her examination.

"You're finally awake, sleepy head." Christian rubs my hair, which I'm sure is looking unruly right now.

"Thanks for letting me rest my head on your shoulder." I smile.

"Anytime, Love." Christian smiles back.

"The doctors haven't said anything yet, right?" I ask.

"No, they haven't, but they said that they'll have the results soon."

"They've been saying that all night." Truth rolls her eyes. She's sitting directly across from Christian and I, and Ava is sitting beside her.

"Where did Micah and Nehemiah go?" I wonder.

"They outside," Ava answers.

"For what?" I ask.

"Fresh air I guess," she responds.

"Has anyone heard from Mercy?" I texted her earlier to let her know that Ryann was at the hospital and to see how she was doing after finding out about Joel, but she never responded to me.

"Nope," Truth replies.

"Did Micah tell Joy that we're here?" I ask.

"I don't know," Truth answers.

"I think he said he was going to call her before he and Nehemiah went outside," Christian says.

"Oh ok," I respond. "I really appreciate you and Nehemiah for staying here with us. I'm sure Ryann appreciates it, too."

"It's no problem." Christian smiles, and I feel those same butterflies I felt when we had our first conversation.

"Aww, how cute!" Ava says.

"Aww what?" Christian asks, still smiling.

"Relationship goals," Ava responds.

"Whatever." I laugh.

"Whatever?" Christian stops smiling and looks at me. Truth and Ava also look at me. "You don't think we're relationship goals?"

I run my hands through my fro. "I didn't know we were in a relationship."

"Would you like to be my girlfriend, Love?"

"Umm..." I begin before the doctor suddenly walks into the waiting room.

"Hi, you guys. Sorry for the wait, but the results of Miss Warner's tests are ready. She requested that you all join her before we read the results to her," she says.

We all get up to follow the doctor to the room where they're keeping Ryann. I'm feeling really nervous because of what Christian just asked me and because the look on Dr. Smith's face doesn't look too good.

When we make it to Ryann's room, she is sitting alone on the bed watching a program on ESPN. She looks calm, but I pray the news we're about to receive doesn't change that.

"Are you ready to hear your results, Miss Warner?" Dr. Smith asks.

"Hold on," Ryann says. "Love, can you pray first?"

"Yes, I can." I nod my head and place my hand on Ryann's leg. "Dear Lord, we come to You as humbly as we know. Lord, we really need You right now. Our dear friend and sister, Ryann, is hurting right now, but we know that You are a comforter and healer. I pray You move through Ryann's life in a supernatural way right now. I pray that You give her the strength to accept the results of the tests, no matter what they may be. We know that You have a purpose and a plan for everything that You allow to happen to us. Help us to remember that. In Jesus' name, amen."

"Amen," everyone says, including Micah and Nehemiah who walked in during the middle of the prayer.

"Thank you for that beautiful prayer, young lady. Shall I proceed?" Dr. Smith asks.

"Yes, go ahead," Ryann says. "Hold my hands, y'all."

"Ok," I say before softly grasping her hand. Truth grabs the other, and Ava puts her hand on Ryann's shoulder.

"I have good news and bad news," Dr. Smith says. "Which do you want first?"

"What's the good news?" Ryann asks.

"The good news is that you don't have any life-threatening injuries."

"What's the bad news then?" Ryann looks more concerned than she did at first.

"The bad news is that you have a broken left leg and a torn anterior cruciate ligament." All of the boys in the room cringe.

"Is that bad?" Ava asks.

"So, you mean to tell me that my leg is broken and my ACL is torn?" Ryann asks in disbelief.

"Yes, I'm sorry," Dr. Smith responds.

"When will I be healed?" Ryann asks, tears forming in her eyes.

"I will admit that the recovery process for this type of injury can be lengthy, and you will need to have surgery to repair your ACL."

"When will it be healed?" Ryann raises her voice. "When will I be able to play basketball again?"

"The healing process can take anywhere between six months to a year."

"You've got to be kidding me! That's the whole basketball season!"

"I'm sorry, sweetheart." Dr. Smith pulls out copies of Ryann's x-rays. "This is what we're dealing with here."

"Lord." Micah shakes his head, and I see why. Ryann's injury looks pretty bad.

"How soon should she have surgery?" Truth asks.

"As soon as possible," Dr. Smith answers.

Soon after, Dr. Smith leaves us alone with Ryann. No one can seem to find the words to say right now to console Ryann as she begins to cry uncontrollably.

"Let's look to God," Nehemiah says before beginning to pray over Ryann.

After Nehemiah is done praying, the rest of us take turns praying for Ryann. Truth and I even sing a few uplifting spiritual hymns. Hopefully all of this praying and singing makes her feel a little bit better.

On the way from the hospital, Micah, Truth, Ava, and Ryann ride together, me and Christian ride together, and Nehemiah drives home alone. It has been such a long and eventful day, and I can't wait to get home, shower, pray, and go to sleep.

"Love?" Christian looks at me when he pushes his car to a stop in front of my house.

"Yes?" I look back at him and then out the window again like I was doing before.

"Are you ok?" He caresses my shoulder.

"Yeah, I'm ok."

"Are you sure? You haven't said much since we left the hospital."

"I'm sure." I look at him and place my hand over his hand that's on my shoulder.

"What's going through your head? I'm all ears."

"Everything," I say. "Literally everything is running through my head right now."

"Like what?"

"I really hate that Ryann's season had to start off like this. I also hate what happened to Mercy today, and I hate that she couldn't be there for Ryann. I understand that she's upset with Joel, but I can't help but feel upset that she wasn't there for Ryann tonight."

"Does she know?"

"Her read receipts were on, so I know she saw my messages. Micah said he told Joy to tell her, too, but no one heard a word from her."

"Dang, that's messed up."

"Yeah, I know." I shake my head.

"But you know it's all going to be alright. Don't you?" He rubs my shoulder.

"Yes, I trust that God is going to work all of this out for our good. I just know He is."

"That's right, Love." Christian smiles his beautiful smile at me once again. Having him here to talk to all evening was definitely a blessing from God. I don't know what I would've done without him.

"I should get going now," I say, looking at my watch. It says that it's 1:58am, which is way past my bedtime.

"Wait," Christian says as I place my hand on the door handle. "I need to ask you something."

"What's up?"

"Do you remember what I asked you earlier?"

"When?"

"When we were at the hospital in the waiting room."

After pausing for a moment to think, I reply, "I'm sorry. I don't remember. Can you remind me?" I think I know which question he's talking about, but I'm afraid to admit it.

"Love, I know you've had a long day and I know it's kinda soon, but would you like to be my girlfriend?"

I figured he was going to ask me this again, but I don't know how to respond. Of course, I would love to be his girlfriend, but I don't know if I should say yes right now. Things are going beyond amazing between us, but I feel like it's entirely too soon to be committing to a relationship with him. I have a lot going on in my life with my new internship about to start next week, and I feel like my friends really need me the most right now. I don't want to become too distracted by a relationship that I forget the people closest to me.

"Before you say no, I just want you to know that you're perfect to me. End of story. I want you in my present and my future, and I wish I had you in my past."

"I want you in mine too, Christian," I admit.

"So, is that a yes?" Christian looks hopeful. I don't want to disappoint him, but I feel like I know what I must do right now.

After a long pause, I answer, "No, it isn't a yes."

"Really?" His eyes widen in shock.

"Yes, really," I say. "I would love to be with you, but I don't want us to rush ahead of God. We're still getting to know each other, and I would love for us to continue to gradually grow before we make a major commitment like this. Plus, my friends really need me right now."

"Yeah, I understand. You're right. I don't know why I'm trying to rush things."

"So, you're not mad at me for saying no?"

"Not at all." Christian laughs. "I guess I was just trying to snatch you up before someone else did."

"You don't have to worry about that. Guys don't really talk to me like that," I respond.

"They don't know what they're missing, but I do. You're someone worth waiting for."

"Really?"

"Yes, really." Christian grabs my hand. "Just promise me you won't fall for anyone else. Ok?"

"Ok." I smile before exiting Christian's car. He rushes to my side to walk me to the front door.

Once we make it to the door, he says, "I guess this is good night."

"I guess it is, too. Good night, Christian."

"Good night, my Love." He reaches out to hug me, and I hug him back.

"I'll see you at school tomorrow."

"Yeah, see you at school tomorrow." Christian flashes his dimples before leaving me alone.

Dear Lord, despite everything that's going on right now, thank You for this tiny bit of perfection. Amen.

***

About the Author

Briuana Green is currently a senior at Harvard College studying Psychology. She was born and raised in Forrest City, Arkansas. Her motivation for writing is to help the youth realize that there is purpose embedded within them, despite what goes on around them. When not writing, Briuana loves spending time with Jesus, family, and friends. She also enjoys reading, sleeping, cheerleading, watching sports (#CowboysNation #GoSpursGo), and endlessly scrolling through social media. Feel free to email her at briuana_green@yahoo.com.

Made in the USA
Lexington, KY
07 August 2018